doppelgänger

2001: A Space Odyssey – about brain death?
                    p. 52 – about rebirth

Like Frankenstein – p. 57

If   surgery is violence, then violence =
                                    rebirth for

THE TRANSPLANT MEN Gus

p. 8 "extraordinary for something once the portland."
p. 9 "no doubt he was not harmed ..."

THE TRANSPLANT MEN

Jane Taylor

This edition published by Jacana Media (Pty) Ltd in 2009

10 Orange Street
Sunnyside
Auckland Park 2092
South Africa
+2711 628 3200
www.jacana.co.za

ISBN 978-1-77009-716-2

Set in Ehrhardt 11/14pt
Printed by Pinetown Printers, KwaZulu-Natal
Job No. 000992

See a complete list of Jacana titles at www.jacana.co.za

Adam Smith,
Two Notes on Biography:

By the imagination we place ourselves in his situation, we conceive ourselves enduring all the same torments, we enter as it were into his body, and become in some measure the same person with him, and thence form some ideas of his sensations. – *The Theory of Moral Sentiments*

The wear and tear of a slave, it has been said, is at the expense of his master; but that of a free servant is at his own expense. – *The Wealth of Nations*

Part One

EACH SUICIDE IS UNIQUE. It often stands as the major achievement of the life which precedes it. Three years ago I was called in to assess a particularly interesting case after a mutilated body was discovered in a house that appeared to have been secured from inside. How did the perpetrator enter the premises bypassing the security system and leaving no sign of a forced entry? That was the pressing question, because the first suspicion was that the man had been the victim of some botched murder or satanic ritual. Both are pretty commonplace now, the stock in trade of police-work. Unlike suicides, in other words, most murders are indistinguishable.

Once intrusion was ruled out, it then became evident that the scalpel found at the scene must have been wielded by the hand of the victim, who bled to death after attempting to disembowel himself. Presumably he was unconscious some time before he died, because a large quantity of benzodiazepine was found in his system.

I was called early on in the investigation, to help with the assessment of the man's state of mind. Was it likely that he had taken his own life? In those initial weeks the finding was still unresolved. During this period I came across the complex archive of materials which he had amassed presumably as some kind of narrative account of his actions. Here was a fascinating case of a man who had blurred the boundaries between the elements of his life, as if event and story were somehow indistinguishable for him. The documents were significant for that alone. More than this, though, they provided the trace of a particular episode in world history which, for complex reasons, has not received the attention which is its due.

At the centre of this account is one of the most intense and profound of human dramas, which could not fail to be metaphoric. Curiously, though, the story here is told not by any of the primary protagonists involved. Rather it has been narrated by a witness who allowed himself to be drawn into events through an act of observation. Increasingly that is our relationship to

3

history. We feel its force because we have received a persuasive report.

From that personal archive I have assembled the papers and the video recordings of Guy Hawthorne. They may be of interest to those who are still curious about the origins of our modernity in this country. My own interest arises from a purely scholarly fascination with the history of anatomy. This record can be trusted. I am one of those unlikely men who from some kind of inner compulsion keep a written record of even such events as might implicate them. On occasion I perhaps have presumed too much knowledge of the author, who at one time had consulted me professionally. I have kept my editorial comments to a minimum, in order not to contaminate the evidence, as it were. The first text is a transcription of the main video tape, including a literal description of its visual elements.

Trans

1:

"I AM NOT GENERALLY WHAT one would call a ready advocate. I avoid taking sides. But now and again I am compelled, from what seems to me a misrepresentation, or a distortion of facts as I know them to be, to state the case as I understand it."

He looks at the bundle of papers rather anxiously, rearranges several sheaths which are held together with an assortment of clips, and begins by quietly reading an epigraph, almost as a way of clearing his throat.

"The heart has reasons of which the reason knows not."

After a pause of some seconds, he adds the attribution.

"Pascal."

He smiles lightly, possibly taking comfort from the authority of the name. Then his faltering start becomes an increasingly steady flow of words.

"The account which I am about to give is not altogether coherent, but then neither am I. For some forty years I have been dependent on a transplanted organ which sustains my existence. There are others whose life story mirrors that of a nation; mine, however, coincides with the history of a medical technology. It is a startling and in many ways a glamorous tale. Happily I have kept an extensive record of much which others may have lost."

Out of the corner of his vision he is vaguely aware of a red light, the eye of a recording device looking back at him. It disconcerts him. Or rather, it concerts him, as his mode becomes increasingly theatrical.

"History is an allegory of giving and taking. As a result it seems that an incalculable debt has been laid at my door, for which I will have to pay. There is no use protesting that it was my own brother whose exceptional gift afforded me an extended life. In the abstract record of obligations, someone has kept a note, and against my name in that invisible book is the defining legend: Guy Hawthorne. Recipient."

5

Pause. With a slight shaking of his head he reconsiders what now feels to him like a false start.

"Those comments had seemed a sufficient beginning. Are they adequate to an ending?"

Mentally, he shuffles again through the papers, tests an arrangement of ideas. When he begins once more, he has the flawless execution of an Olympic diver as he flings himself into his first tumble.

2:

"MY FIRST CONCERN IS WITH the complex legacy of my friend, Chris Barnard. It is not necessary to make him more than he was in order not to make him less than he was. My hope is that through this account we might come to reassess the role which he played in the story of ourselves. He stands as a special type of Afrikaner on the cusp of South African modernity. I don't pretend to fully grasp what that means. But I sense that he is less significant for us in Africa than for his place in world history. I am inclined to say, in a sweeping gesture, that 'that is often the way'. However, it seems as true that 'this is seldom the case'.

"Chris's inspiration has led me to where I am. It was inevitable that we would become entangled. Some scepticism there may be about the link between us, but let me assure you that I would suffer almost anything before willingly drawing him into a sordid controversy. I write as a fan. Let that be clear. Still, I have no interest in justifying either him or myself. We have seen a great deal of that in the past decades.

"It is more important that the record be accurate with regard to his place in history, rather than with my own. This is not false modesty. Mine is not a straightforward narrative about a man with a unified idea of himself or his life. There are distinctive circumstances which may account for this. The one who acts is not necessarily the same as the one who gives account of that action.

"No doubt any man is composed of several parts. The jumble holds together somehow through combinations that are ever-changing. Many treatises in both poetry and prose have been written about revolutions in the realm of ideas; literature explores how the passions, too, are subject to periodic upheaval. Organic change – yes. *King Lear* will tell us about the process of ageing, but changing organs —? Almost nothing tells us about the significance of the transplant.

"We did not understand how it would leave us all undefended. This is not to say that sickness is a metaphor. Rather, it is health that is metaphorical. Oh yes. Because from the start we are infected with that which will kill us. And yet we assert (how many times a day?) 'fine, thank you, fine'.

"Over the past three hundred years the public stood by watching while the interpretation of the body was transferred out of the realm of art and into the sphere of science. Only a small community remained in touch with the body's meanings. So incremental has been the sea change that we scarcely perceived it. For the general population, it is as if we had sought to observe, from one of a pair of twin islands in a tropical bay, the events taking place on the island some thousands of yards away. Perhaps we have seen a hand waving, and have hailed or hallooed in return, only to discover that it was just a palm frond swaying in an unusual breeze.

"Several decades ago, I was part of — what? — a historical shift? We were a generation of scholars who believed that we could advance the total circumstance of the human being. So it was that I began to undertake the research which led to my personal encounter with the surgeon who performed the first successful human heart transplant, Dr Christiaan Barnard.

"That was how I thought of him then. It was a moment when we were extraordinary for something other than Apartheid. Chris represented hope. His work triggered events that would dominate my life and bring about a change in me.

"Oh, yes, Baaarnard!' a friend says with a drawl. 'He was a real showman.'

"It's not that I disagree, but if we regard the episode in this light we will fail to explore its real significance.

"Easy opinion has of late dismissed the first heart transplant as a piece of facile exhibitionism. But a revolution of ideas took place in that operating theatre; new passions were stirred. That's what I want to say. We began a journey which has turned the world inside out.

"Remarkable times are often tainted by the banal. As a result the surgeon who for such a time was on everybody's lips for a miraculous achievement has now largely disappeared from memory and what lingers, at worst, is a question about the legitimacy of his personal lifestyle; at best it challenges us about the legitimacy of the transplant as a medical procedure.

"From the start, people tried to interpret his motives as well as his achievements. 'Why had he done it?' was almost as important as 'how had he done it?' All of that speculation added to the controversy.

8

"No doubt he was not normal. How would an ordinary man scoop a beating heart out of the chest of one human being, in order to determine whether it would power another's body? 'That's witchcraft, not science.' Certainly I was initially terrified by his audacity. No doubt, doubt gnawed at my soul. Surely Chris could not have had common inhibitions or appetites? Decency imposes its own constraints on the imagination. Thank God.

"My mother always thought that a fair proportion of Barnard's genius lay in his beauty. Chris would have been striking in any gathering, even without his remarkable celebrity. One could be forgiven for inferring that his portion was well above that of other men. He was tall and lean in the elegant way of Fred Astaire, or James Steward, and his bearing was always upright, like an exclamation mark. Barnard's generation hadn't yet learned to admit that men might be self-regarding, and so in spite of his good looks, in the early years he seemed to be almost careless of his appearance. Of course, nothing could be further from the truth as we learned when he got older. He valued physical perfection intensely.

"I myself am just below average height, and while I am not unattractive, no one would consider me handsome. As such things go, I am almost invisible. Nonetheless I was able to forge a privileged relationship of affection with this man who belonged so absolutely to the world, this rather beautiful man who was a combination of poetry and the prosaic."

Speaking these words, he is very conscious of the video camera. Is his jacket too modest, or too assertive? He should have worn a shirt and tie rather than the polo neck. He had not considered that this would be his one chance at immortality.

These thoughts are unspoken but seem evident to me through a slight alteration in his physical attitude. He draws himself up, while dropping his shoulders an inch or so. For a moment he is viewing himself as the camera sees him. The signs are minimal, yet I understand them. I understand him.

"Chris's fame might have deterred another kind of man from pursuing a relationship with him. It would these days. Celebrity has become a *sine qua non* for us. It raises boundaries between us, and those who are extraordinary exist in a realm of their own. Back then it never occurred to me that I might not be of interest to him. That's what happens when you grow up in a small country. Unconsciously I assumed that I could have access to almost anyone. Based on this, I was brash enough to contact an individual who was already one of the most famous figures of our era. Perhaps that had merit, because here you are following the reflections of myself, a nobody. At this late hour, is it merely my relationship with him that you want to understand? It was simple. Our enjoyment of one another arose from the fact that we were both fascinated by him. Not even Washkansky's death could diminish Chris's appeal.

"For the sake of anyone unfamiliar with the name of Louis Washkansky, he was the man whose change of heart brought Barnard international renown. More directly stated, in December 1967, Chris sewed the heart of Denise Darvall inside the chest of Washkansky. You would have been hard-pressed to find anyone who did not know this back then, because it was heralded as the first. Not Louis, not Denise, nor Chris would ever be the same again.

"The operation divided international medical opinion on Barnard. Several saw him as the harbinger of the new. Many thought him a sensationalist. Some called for him to be deregistered. One influential colleague stigmatised him as a talented psychopath. None was indifferent.

"My first meeting with him was brief, at the funeral of Clive Haupt. Clive was the second South African heart donor. That was in 1968. There was such a crush of people that I just once got the opportunity to touch his sleeve. I remember that he did nod . . ."

Hawthorne looks uneasy, and a momentary pause follows, as he considers how to proceed. His head twitches once to the left, a tiny motion that is probably more visible on video than it would be in the ebb and flow of everyday life, where the overall impression of his calm intelligence would dominate.

"I'm sorry, I'll read that again."

He winces when he recognises the well-worn phrase he has produced, which moreover has resonances of comic pastiche. His hand imperceptibly removes the folded square of a white handkerchief briefly from his pocket, and invisibly returns it. He glances up from his papers, and then provides a brief spontaneous interjection that takes the form of a gloss or commentary on his own words.

"I realise that my previous sentence should read 'did not' rather than 'did nod'. In fact I don't think that Chris actually greeted me. Certain people can affirm your existence simply through their presence. Sometimes a beautiful woman can have the same effect, when she affectionately takes your hand as she shares a confidence. My recollection is that his eyes suggested a momentary flicker of recognition. But he of course was mistaken. Perhaps he took me for the son of a family friend, or a boyfriend of his daughter. After which he seemed to realise his mistake and turned away. I still puzzle over what it was in me that Chris recognised. Nonetheless, the funeral was one of the great events of my life."

He turns back to his notes.

"Even now the entire Haupt saga remains remarkable. Defying prevailing attitudes, Chris had taken the heart of a coloured man, and had used it to fill the meticulously prepared cavity within the chest of a retired Jewish dentist, Philip Blaiberg. Haupt's community celebrated Barnard for ignoring race, so that even though it was Clive Haupt who had been the donor, the outpouring of gratitude was such that it seemed at the time as if Barnard was the gift-giver.

"While it was unusual in those days, it was not *unsafe* for a white lad to move through coloured society. Effie, our domestic servant, was herself of mixed African and coloured descent and she colluded in persuading my mother to let me go to the funeral in Salt River. Once or twice she said something which made me believe that she felt sorry for a young man who had recently lost his twin brother.

"Of course we project ourselves into others, and I imagined Effie herself had some interest in following these procedures through which a coloured man's heart had ended up inside a white man's chest. That may have been a misperception born of those times. Perhaps it was whites who were obsessed by race back then.

"Mother was not fully aware of how closely I was following the saga. I had just finished my matric exams and was in that agitated tedium which precedes the shift from school to university. The normal trajectory in those days would have been military service because conscription had just been introduced. I, however, had been exempted on medical grounds. The urgency of my desire to attend Haupt's funeral seemed to distress Mother. She sought comfort from family friends.

"'The boy has developed a taste for death,' she muttered to Uncle Enoch who had come round for dinner. He had been a regular at the house once my father disappeared. After coffee he sought me out where I was drawing

11

in the study. I remember him as simple and honest, qualities not much valued by an adolescent boy in a melancholic state.

"'What's this about going to a funeral?' he asked. 'Of someone you don't even know? A coloured chappie?'

"I held my sketch book up to him.

"'And what's that?' he enquired. 'It's very good, but what the hell is it?'

"'It's a fence,' I responded. Then I added, darkly, 'It's a hole in a fence. Death is a hole in a fence.'

"There is real value in being able to scare an adult when you are eighteen."

At this point the recorded interview terminates. It is a great frustration to me that the intimacy of that spoken history is so limited in extent. There are one or two additional recordings which are not central to the case, and so they have not been transcribed here. Nonetheless these have no doubt also influenced my understanding as editor.

In addition to our minimal early contact, those materials perhaps have determined in some way the choices I have made in putting together this material. I regret the incompleteness of the video-memoir which is something of a novelty. Presumably Hawthorne's original intention had been to read the entire transcription of his narrative, doing the police in different voices, as it were. Some factor must have prompted him to terminate that plan. The remainder of the record exists only as an unusually detailed written document which is at times fragmentary and somewhat oblique. A reader can now only imagine what might have been the impact of a fully recorded and performed event.

Any gaps or incompleteness must be understood for what they can tell us about the state of his mind at the end. The record has been produced in a great outpouring over a period of some three weeks; at times it seems a torrent. On occasion remarkably detailed and personal, frequently remote and clinical, Hawthorne's memoir gives us access to his own distinctive imagination, as he reconstructs the historical events which he observed so closely. Few people have scrutinised the early years of the transplant as carefully as he did. We should not distrust his analysis simply because he happened to be both a witness and a subject of that history. Much of what we now have taken as our historical archive is based on just such testimony.

A large portion of his record arises from events which took place decades ago now, long before our historic transformation in this country, and must be read in that light. My objective had originally been to proceed without revealing too early what was to be the ghastly outcome. Such prefiguring can give a life the sense of being predestined. We would cease to see what was of interest and engagement in the ordinary circumstances of Hawthorne's existence, and everything would come to be read in terms of the final weeks in which he made those momentous choices. But actually much of the interest in these documents is that there is no obvious sign that the writer foresaw his destiny. There are certain preoccupations, of course, but the whole is not dominated by the ending, except in the mind of that reader with foreknowledge. Despite this I have been persuaded by the publishers that it is as well to give the reader some understanding of the significance of what they read, without which the book would have no drama, much like ordinary existence. Endings shape beginnings and so we read, as it were, backwards.

I trust that you will not be so engaged by the story of Guy Hawthorne that Barnard will disappear from your mind's eye. Similarly my hope is that you will not become so interested in the life of Chris Barnard that you lose sight of Guy Hawthorne.

I don't wish to prejudice the reader's interpretation, but it is my sense that Hawthorne was in the main governed by the keenest psychological motives. He was driven to make reparation for the undeserved gift he had received. A straightforward anonymous solicitation from a donor organisation became, in his case, an absolute compulsion, almost a persecutory demon.

This is not in the usual sense of the word a "confession" although at times we are aware of a man trying to understand the whole which has arisen from the sum of his parts. Hawthorne asks how much he needs to tell in order to clean the slate without having to disclose matters which remain secret even to himself. So in certain respects his record is unbelievably detailed, while on other matters his life remains a closed book.

World history suggests that there are, on one side of a great divide, those to whom "much has been given". From such, we are told, much will be expected.

Finally, it is important for the reader to bear in mind that the first person voice in the following pages is his, and not mine.

3:

SOME SIXTEEN MONTHS AFTER the Haupt funeral, and with no other way of re-establishing contact with Chris, I determined to telephone him. Sometimes that is all that it takes to divert the course of your life. Change doesn't always arrive like a runaway train racing down a snow-clad mountain pass. The phone call was the first substantial contact in what was to become one of the most significant relationships in my life. Many of my recent choices have arisen from that initial encounter, one way or another. It may be a difficult fact to grasp, but when my brother died I felt as if I had lost my compass. Some days I did not have the energy to swing my legs out of bed, to place my feet on the floor, to pivot my weight and lever myself into an upright position. A great dullness would weigh upon me like an eagle on my chest. The idea of contacting Chris became an absolute objective. He was my idol. I was scarcely more than a child, and was unaware of the phrase "feet of clay".

It was surprisingly easy to track down his phone number through only a slight misrepresentation at the hospital. I was put through to his office by the hospital switchboard. While I waited for him to answer I listened to the tones of the telephone, clacking and purring in my ear like a foreign being.

Then at last, there he was.

I was shocked to hear his high-pitched and unhappily rather feeble voice. It seemed strangely at odds with the piercing eyes and radiant smile so familiar from press photos. Nature is at times rather eccentric in her distribution of gifts. Of course, I'd heard him on the radio but had managed to persuade myself that there was some deficiency in the recording process which distorted what he sounded like. Even at nineteen I had the sonorous tones of a man much taller and older than myself.

"How do you get organs donated?" was the first question I asked him. Because I was inexperienced I went straight to the heart of the matter. We talked back and forth a little. Then he interrupted me with something that was clearly obsessing him. Clearly, while he was talking to me, he really was in a dialogue with himself. A dialogue can often be the pretext for a monologue.

"The real problem that we still haven't solved is rejection. Even now, with the tissue-typing lab and everything, we still can't stop the immune system from attacking the new organ."

Reconsidering this exchange all these years later, it still seems strange to me as a layman that no one has considered the link between immune suppression and the recent history of immunodeficiency. Transplant teams the world over set about undermining the human immune system. Have millions died of AIDS so that thousands could live with transplants? Of course not. That's a paranoid question. Yet progress takes no prisoners.

I was always rather anxious about these questions, and have tried to consider the ethics of the matter. Naturally a boy who has had a transplant understands these questions in his own way.

"Surgery is not public health. Surgeons operate on individuals." That remains my interpretation.

Still, back then I was not engaged by these larger issues. Many of us allowed such matters to go unexamined. The transplant seemed to be a "natural" evolution within the surgical field. And surgery was a natural evolution of anatomical understanding. We were all renaissance men.

When I recall my conversation with Chris I realise that childishly I was worrying not so much about what he was saying, as about his voice. Because I myself was verging on manhood, it concerned me that my idol sounded so feeble. His voice seemed not to belong to the impressive figure I had seen both in the flesh and on the news. If not from the voice, where did a man get his power? That's what the twentieth century taught us.

Then the conversation turned to his concerns and not mine. Chris feared being overshadowed by surgeons working in better-equipped and better-funded institutions abroad.

"They've got the money! They've got the time!" He would *not* allow himself to be eclipsed.

I found myself wanting to support him. "We'll always remember Edmund Hillary as The First," I insisted. On reconsideration I can see how strange that conversation was. I was exhorting a world-renowned stranger almost thirty years my senior. That is an unlikely role for a nineteen-year-old.

"Your achievement is all the greater for being accomplished from Cape Town," I said in response to his complaint that the world was catching up. "It will signal that our country is thriving." In those days I did not align myself with the nay-sayers who were making so much fuss in the aftermath of the Terrorism Act.

"You are our sputnik." I spoke in a florid set of comparisons, as I often do when seized by an enthusiasm. I wasn't exaggerating. "Our Yuri Gagarin."

Barnard snorted. It was almost a bray. He sounded less than pleased. The Soviets had made great scientific breakthroughs, some of which Chris had observed firsthand, as you will learn. But they too had had their setbacks. In April 1967 Vladimir Komarov had died when *Soyuz 1* slammed into the earth on re-entry. The Soviets were trying to dock capsules within one another in outer space. Was this dream inspired by their own experiments with transplant, or rather, did surgery mimic space travel? I cannot believe that these were unrelated systems, as you will see later from my research.

Soviet breakthroughs were shrouded in secrecy back then because they were pariahs to the West, particularly to the Americans. I wonder how Chris would feel if he were alive to see where we have all come. Who are the pariahs now?

I heard him out for a while, on who was misguided and the general public. Then I could contain myself no longer.

"How can I live with my brother inside me?" It was a crass and blunt question, poorly formulated.

"Your brother?" His tone was startled. Then I told him about my own transplant. At once his voice was electric with appetite, and his tongue became a scalpel. What, who, why?

"A kidney," I elaborated in response to his queries. "Three years ago. From my twin brother."

A small gasp cut through the distance between us as Chris breathed in sharply through his teeth. "Ah, yes. I remember. Hawthorne. You were lucky. To have a twin," he mused. "My brother had a twin who died."

There was a pause as if he was reconsidering what he had said, followed by a burst of easy laughter and then,

"My *older* brother, Barney. He was a twin, but his sister died. So obviously, they weren't identical. I lost a brother too, from a heart defect. Klein Abraham. My father once showed me a Marie biscuit he kept that had the little chap's teeth marks on it. If your brother saved you, you owe him. You two were identical. I remember the case."

Because this dialogue took place on the phone I couldn't see his expression, but I was aware of the earnestness in his voice. He knew me. Chris often used platitudes, but his tone was always sincere. My own comments tend to the bookish, as a consequence of my sequestered boyhood.

"It is no longer within my remit to repay," was my response. "My brother died a few years after the surgery, in a car crash. But I still sometimes wonder whether *I* was the one who died. You see, I feel, sometimes —"

"Yes?' he interjected. "You feel . . . ?"

His voice was taut with interest and animation.

"I feel as if that kidney of his, as if it's more myself than the rest of me."

How could I explain to him what I experience? At first it was nothing, just the standard physical discomfort after surgery. When I went to sleep at night, I would find myself unconsciously running my finger across the scar in a gesture of physical consolation. As the pain diminished, I became more rather than less aware of the new organ, until I persuaded myself that my kidney functions had ceased to be involuntary. I am advised by both my doctor and my therapist that this is an illusion, but it is of such substance that I can't ignore it or will it away. With Viv's death, that sensation only became more present to me.

How difficult is the decision to donate a kidney in order to save a life? I wanted to know. Possibly my exaggerated estimation of Barnard's significance was because I owe my life to my brother's kidney. Could he help me to understand what it had meant to live with my brother alive inside me?

In the first year after the surgery, despite the facts of the matter, it felt not as if Viv was inside me, but rather that I was inside him. That now scarcely seems possible, and was a surprise to Chris. I tried to explain it. My brother had always been the harbour which had given shelter to my storm-tossed little being. He was my suit of armour.

"Can you explain the increased attention which the kidney has begun to demand now that Viv is dead?" I asked.

To some it may seem strange that I approached a heart surgeon on the matter of the kidney. While cardiac surgery did provide Chris with the pinnacle of his professional success, I have always believed that his real specialty was not so much the heart as *the transplant*. You will appreciate the significance of that difference. By then Barnard had become so completely identified with the heart that the public was already largely unaware that he had been a pioneer of renal surgery in this country.

"You performed the first kidney transplant at Groote Schuur Hospital, is that right?" was an early question, although I knew the answer. That query was just a ruse. Flatter him. Surprise him. Most people were only

17

interested in the story of the heart. Get him to tell you about the episode in his own words.

"That's right," he responded. "I had a one hundred percent success with kidneys."

Although that fact is impressive, it was disappointing to hear him say it. I had read the comment more than once before. Of course, it was true. Chris only ever did the one kidney transplant, as a way of training the team for the cardiac op. But his formulaic response to me was quick and pat, and it felt like a dismissal. I couldn't bear it that he was treating me as a member of the public, to be flattered and toyed with. I have learned how to work my way through such initial impediments, through obstinacy. I could not let our conversation founder. These were the contradictory feelings he aroused within me from the start.

We despise the kidney because it seems to be little more than a sewer. But it is purifying the blood that the heart pushes around the system. What use is a new heart without a viable kidney? I did not speak these ideas out loud. Chris after all had said many times that the heart was just a pump. Still, he knew all along that it was also the centre of a great romance.

Our dialogue faltered once or twice, and we fell back into awkward silences and stilted questions. My awe was at odds with his indifference, although at times he was using all of the seductive charm that he lavished on the media man. What had the heart op taught him that he hadn't already known?

"We learned so bloody much so bloody quick," was his reply. I must have responded because my notebook indicates that he then elaborated slightly. His comments were well rehearsed and the pace assured. (These were my observations at the time. My invalid years had made me a prodigious note-taker, using a method of my own devising.)

"Some of it was technical, okay: the temperature of the body; also how it's best to remove the old heart leaving a small cuff in place to attach the new one. Don't get rid of the whole thing. That's the real trick. But there was also coping with the stress. You must be sure and accurate. And don't hesitate. You have to just keep going until it's done. Like in a abattoir. You can't decide *sommer* halfway that you don't want to kill the calf. He'll kick you. He'll try to escape, if he knows you have doubt. I remember watching on the farms when I was just a *pikkie*. Before they even start with the business, you want them to stop. But once they begin, all you want is for them to kill it. Finish and *klaar*. You must go through with it; do the whole thing."

18

4:

IT IS APPROPRIATE HERE TO consider the impact of my relationship with Barnard on later incidents. Most of my life I have avoided commitments. So it is now rather unclear to me quite how I embarked upon a project that has tied my soul absolutely to a series of formal obligations. I am trying to understand how my current situation has arisen in relation to past choices and fixations. Perhaps my needs would have remained submerged if it had not been for a recent triggering event. Simply because of a personalised letter from a service network calling themselves POST/OP, the whole of my history has returned to me with force. POST/OP had my details in a databank and had obviously been given the record that I was one of the receivers, as I call us.

POST/OP position themselves as a recipients' support group, and they provide information and bio-medical advice for post-transplant patients. Inside the envelope that they sent me was a printed pamphlet (POST/OP Care). A personal address, a printed pamphlet. I was both anonymous and individual. That is increasingly the way. This piqued my interest and I tried to find out more about how they knew about me. I checked for their details on the web but there seems to be no digital site, although there are one or two similar addresses. These prove (apparently) to have no link to the organisation that contacted me.

Once they had located me, within weeks I was being inundated with unsolicited information about after-care. Advising me on the problems of rejection and incompatibility, they sent me statistics about immune research. Clearly their records did not indicate the somewhat unique circumstances of my surgery and my brother's donation, which would have indicated my own immunity. Inevitably, there were appeals for organ donors. "A donor is sought . . ." The words struck me as imperatives.

Don't misunderstand me. No actual papers were signed. That is beside the point. My obligation arises from an ethical rather than a legal contract.

I made an offer: to help them to find a donor "within the year". "Donation" is the term used from the early days of the transplant, when it was a matter of conscience, rather like alms for the poor. Since my own transplant some forty years ago, the trade in body parts has been entirely transformed. Viv and I never imagined that our radically redistributed selves could arise from anything but a gift. The talk is still of "donors" and "recipients" although I suspect that everywhere in the world now each organ – and some other parts besides – can be given a monetary value. It is largely a one-way traffic. Arms from the poor.

Draw an outline of a cow. You will find that it is possible to imagine pencilling in a price tag attached to pretty well any of its choice cuts: ribs, loin, flank, shin. A mental drawing of ourselves requires a different kind of map, one which once used to define the internal systems: musculature, veins and arteries, skeleton, organs of reproduction. Now the kidneys, the liver, corneas, heart, femur, a kneecap or two, even the skin, all have become separable provinces. It is the Balkanisation of the human body.

Sometimes the transplanted organ is seamlessly integrated into the body, but on occasion it persists as an outsider, stubbornly remains an archive, refusing to be integrated into the narrative of another. I don't raise these issues in order to defend my choices. Who amongst us can justify what we do? Nor do I intend to impugn POST/OP, which is, I am sure, a legitimate and, god knows, a vital organisation.

"You have been selected . . ." the letter instructed me. Some people are immune to calculated seductions. They succumb neither to the clearing-house sweepstakes, nor to the guaranteed win, nor to the insurance upgrade. Such is not my personality. I cannot resist the appeal which summons me up out of nowhere. Perhaps my modestly religious upbringing prepared me to anticipate messages from the ether, despite my own resolute agnosticism.

". . . because of your unique understanding of what it means to owe your life to the gift of love. Remarkably, organ donation often means that the gift has come to you from a total stranger."

I scrutinised the envelope to see if there was any sign of who might have told on me. The letter itself contained several direct and confrontational questions, in a large typeface, and set inside quotation marks. Grammatically irrelevant, these formulae were inserted rather randomly, communicating a feeling of immediacy, of candour:

Do you thank your donor every day? –

The Gift of Life is Forever. –

Take care of yourself. You OWE it to your donor.

I have no sense of how long I stared at those words. The oblique accusation struck directly into my soul. Some minutes later – who could say how many? – from where I stood in the kitchen, I became aware of what I assumed was the sound of water spilling over the lip of the bath on to the tile floor. A soft flushing noise. Since then, the gentle sensation of some wave-action a little distance removed has been perpetually with me. Did the noise arise from somewhere internal or external to myself? It was strangely disorienting, as it is when you hear a stereo sound inside a pair of headphones and mistake the source of the sound for the Real. Momentarily I thought it might be an aural hallucination.

Now, all these years later, I am clear. The liquid swish-swash was my brother Viv's kidney perpetually at its task. Not for me the purchased CD with a perpetual stream of sound to lull me at night. Rather, I go to sleep with a constant reminder of the thankless labour that my brother's organ undertakes on my behalf. It has become an advocate of all the great inner industry that sustains me. Doorways swing open while others are slammed shut in the washing and flushing and digesting fury of sustaining my life.

Involuntary actions. As if there was a slave population within us who only very rarely makes demands or goes on strike seeking better working conditions. Most of the time we are not even aware of this labour, nor as a rule do we hear our own internal activities ongoing. Only during awkward moments at the opera or, say, an exhibition opening, are we alerted by a low rumbling complaint, a comic explosion.

The inner ear does not advise us of what it hears. And my outer ear listens not to this private symphony. Rather, it is tuned to the universe beyond myself. How is it that I wake to the thrush or the robin, but cannot hear my own heart? The softest creak on the stairs or the forcing of a backdoor rings out as heraldic enunciations of threat, but the ebb and flow of the tides within me generally remain inaudible. That has always struck me as a miracle.

5:

THE REALITY IS THAT I committed myself to POST/OP. It seemed at the time that if I could help them to secure a kidney, I would cancel my debt. It was not enough to buy one through either the legitimate or illegitimate pathways. If I sought seriously to cancel my debt, I would have to add to the sum of kidneys available. This alone would vouch for the sincerity of my actions. Still, it does not save me even from my own dreams, which are filled with recrimination.

J'Accuse is written in red on my pillow each night that I lay down my head. I am in league with monsters, even though the rational part of me is convinced that a man who arranges the donation of a kidney for renal surgery is not identical to one who, howling at the moon, devours the entrails of his neighbour. A surgeon is not a serial killer, yet our ancestors would have written Chris off as an ally of Count Dracula. He plundered bodies throughout his career. The Defence? It was Science and not Magic. Science magically knows that there is a difference between the two, and it envies its wild sister, because only through magic is metamorphosis possible. The best that Science can offer is a repair. Why does my brother's kidney still remind me daily that I am a foreign country? After some forty years it still seems to long for home.

That's why I contacted Chris. I sought him out to help me understand how it is that the transplanted organ continues to exert such power over me if it is simply a biological procedure. That situation seems extraordinary to you? Have you any comprehension how remarkable it is even to myself? But in what does that self consist when my very being depends for its existence on my brother's transplanted organ? Not only my bodily functions, but the mental universe which I call my self, would cease to exist without that "something else" inside of me. Viv's kidney is a kind of Bantustan which never quite lost the traces of its history. I cannot eat without it. I cannot drink without it. In fact, I cannot even dream without it.

6:

MY BROTHER HAD NEVER REALLY discussed with me how he felt about my getting so vital a part of himself, although he certainly did talk about it with mother. Instead of bringing us closer together, as I had wanted, the surgery seemed to create a barrier between us.

Guilt can take various forms. Sometimes it is evident as an aggressive impulse to claim yet more. In my case I was overcome by the sensation that I had received beyond my share. Viv needed proof that we had a special bond, and became convinced that we could communicate with each other by concentrating on our scars. We had read about experiments with twins and extra-sensory perception. Did we share something even keener because of the transplant? I cannot forget a word of our exchange.

"Guy – ?" Viv was looking up at me from his collection of rubber stamps.

"Mmmm?" My distracted response.

"Can you tell what picture I have in my mind right now?"

"It's a car."

"Yes, but what kind of car?"

How would it ever be possible to decide the basis of our bond? Was it the well-documented communion between twins, or was there something distinctive that linked us after the surgery? By now I have become the victim of his donation. During my conscious hours I am aware of the kidney as a silent servant within me. What began as a sensation shortly after Viv's accident developed into a dark and shadowy presence from that day at Haupt's funeral. On occasion I feel as if one of the maids has quietly entered my study, and is standing just inside the door, as they do, waiting for me to recognise her presence. This impression fills me with a curious shame. What's more, I have begun to feel as if the kidney would cease to function if I forgot about it. It is of no use telling me that when I am asleep, the kidney continues unabated. Also pointless is the attempt to persuade me to ignore its presence.

The organ, as Viv and I had jokingly termed it, has taken on a life of its own and begun to dominate my existence. I began to conflate the person of my brother and the person of the kidney. From this I have developed somewhat eccentric habits which have not gone unnoticed among my immediate social circle.

"I think I'll have a small whiskey for Viv," I will say capriciously at the start of the meal, but by the time we get around to the dessert wine, I am quite capable of sobriety.

"I'd better not." (I assume a reluctant air.) "Got to look after the old kidney."

7:

OF COURSE WITHOUT BARNARD'S pioneering experiments, I would in all likelihood never have been redeemed. My parents could not afford to take me and Viv to one of the metropolitan centres for what was very expensive and, let's face it, experimental surgery. Chris had brought the research home. Although by the time I actually received my kidney transplant, he had moved on to his cardiac work, I still liked to think that he was not unaware of the procedures being done by younger researchers who followed after him. In all likelihood he and his colleagues had discussed me over coffee in the hospital canteen. Perhaps one of them had asked his advice, had shown him a chart. Did his expertise in some way contribute to my remarkable recovery? I hope so. Still, his gaze inside me would have been professional almost to the point of indifference.

I would have to admit that as a young scholar I was sexually envious of this man some twenty-five years older than myself. It was not a sexual jealousy, you should understand. There was no one desired object above all others who was removed from me through his own act of possession. That would have been the more classic triangle. His second wife Barbara and I would have been suited to one another in terms of age. This is a hypothetical reflection because she and I never actually met. Anyhow, I am not particularly attracted to her type. A dressage filly. My brother had met Chris's daughter once at the yacht club, but she was too sporty for my sedentary habits. In the end, it was an abstract quality of sexual allure *in him* that I desired. He was not my object. No. I wanted to have what he had. I identify with powerful men.

My own research was generally an unending pale tedium, interlacing words like dead leaves. Here was a different kind of author, with his hands inside another man's chest. While as a young writer I was transposing epithets and stitching together split infinitives, I pictured him as a type of Frankenstein, trying to breathe life into an inanimate corpse.

"How like a God!"

I wanted him to change my life, too.

It came to me as a lightning flash – you know the kind of thing: a bolt happily strikes the coil attached to the massive switch which controls the generator, and the monster sits upright – anyhow, I had an epiphany. I would become his biographer. That resolution may now seem an irrelevance because of Chris's almost absolute disappearance from public memory. He is all but forgotten in the public imagination, but back then he was, aside from apartheid, the one thing for which we were known in the world. More recently it was Mandela, and then the Truth Commission. The heart transplant seemed for a time to be a natural medium for us here. That is no longer so clear.

The world loved Chris because he was an outsider. Yet ironically he wanted to be inside. Yes, that's true, but it's something more. His need was to be at the centre of the world. It was his great hunger. Perhaps that's what drives all celebrity. And for a time, the centre of the world is where he was, if you look at the awards he received. Those awards are now all at the edge of the universe, in the museum in Beaufort West. Of course, when it suited him, he reminded everyone that he was simply a boy from the Karoo. He was just one generation away from the Boer War (as he would have called it). Yet the cosmetic surgeries, the Italian suits and a cultivated naivety all helped to sustain the myth that he was years, decades even, younger than that.

From where I sit now, there is some melancholy in coming to terms with the fact that I have constructed a life's work out of studying a man who no longer seems to be of historical relevance. Perhaps the whole South African experiment, too, will fade from international attention. Transplant pioneers have been displaced by genetic engineers and we didn't keep up. This is what I suspect on bad days. I keep myself afloat through trying to hold on to the principle that the record itself is of significance, and that one day we will want again to know where the adventure began.

This record can be trusted. I am one of those unlikely men who from some kind of inner compulsion keep a written record of even such events as might implicate.

8:

DO YOU REMEMBER MY description of Barnard's high-pitched falsetto? After my voice broke, I discovered that I had a rich baritone which was well suited to the role of Dr Paul. Dr Paul was a medical hero from the world of radio drama; a Kildare of the airwaves. Now *that* was what a heart surgeon sounded like. I myself have the voice of a man much taller than I am, a fact which suggests that I would have been above average height if my growth had not been retarded because of my kidney problems.

The voice of Dr Paul had provided me with valuable companionship during my ailing childhood. I also remember Dulcie van den Bergh. She was hostess of a radio-magazine show *Hospitaaltyd*, which broadcast letters of comfort and cheer to the bed-ridden. "Dis halfeen. Dis Hospitaaltyd. Daar's 'n lied en 'n glimlag vir jou . . ."

I am not even sure that I knew at the time that the programme was in Afrikaans. What I do know is that it was in the language of the chronically ill. Radio made us all citizens back then, even the bed-ridden. The cheerful jingle chimes inside my head, and I am once again that small boy in an armchair with a crocheted woollen rug over my knees. An invalid's tray perched on the coffee-table beside me has a half-made jigsaw puzzle with a scene of a clipper-ship tossed on a stormy sea. My bookish interests became more defined, alternating between literary and medical adventures. I pored over Edwardian textbooks with black-and-white photographs of children suffering with rickets, or curvature of the spine, or scurvy. How I feared them; how I adored them. I considered them my foundlings.

The current fad for the Emergency Room drama is quite unlike my own boyhood romance with the hospital. In those early years you did not anticipate a miraculous intervention. The common understanding was that long-term suffering formed an aspect of the human condition. Now our expectations have shifted. We imagine that good-looking men and women will discover a cure. An ever-expanding pharmacopoeia and innovative procedures will remove us from protracted misery. A treatment; a cure; a vaccine; anything is possible. Suffering, like polio, will disappear from human experience, or will be relocated offshore. That is the fantasy promoted by American television.

Chris played a part in this account. The human body can be mapped, re-zoned, modified. Surely that's beneficial? New specialisations arise, such as "limb salvage". A good man in California uses radiotherapy to bombard a cancerous limb. His patients "would rather die" than live through an amputation.

The theatre of my mind was filled with lint bandages, kidney-shaped enamel dishes. I became enraptured by the buccaneer surgeons imagining a new heaven, a new earth, and I gazed in wonder at the clear blue eyes which radiated Compassion from above the surgical mask. Even now antiseptic is one of my favourite perfumes, and its acrid sweetness exceeds magnolia blossom, instilling a feeling of opulent calm in my soul.

It is misguided to assume that the years I spent under chronic medical care must have been filled with anxiety. On the contrary. I sensed reassurance and support in those interventionist environments. The dedication of the professional once was substantial. Care was not distrusted just because paid for. Rather, it was the banal spaces of domestic life which, despite parental love, left me feeling undefended. My mother's enduring sense of incompetence in the face of my illness must surely have coloured my recollections. There we were, tied to one another by our ignorance. She did what she could, and pieces of information, which travelled slowly and singly in those days, arrived in sealed envelopes via a circulatory system that was sclerotic.

This is not simply my story; it is Chris's too. I find that I cannot justify his ways without explaining a full system of related meanings. Several of those who have attempted to capture these events were inadequate to the task. There are one or two fine histories of the surgical history, but his personal narrative is usually poorly served. Worse, he was encouraged to stray into lurid anecdote, and so I hold his writers responsible for much of his negative legacy. Throughout his life Chris had an unhappy craving for fame, immortality and financial reward, factors that made him vulnerable to exploitation. No celebrity is immune. It is part of the contract.

I am at times frustrated that I didn't ever have the opportunity to work more directly with him. Imagine standing poised with a living human organ inside your hand, the old not yet dead, and the new still about to come into being. The common image once was "the birth of a nation", but our modernity is not well served by that metaphor.

Birth is no longer the most ordinary of processes, and a lifespan is not limited by nature. Body parts circulate and allow for a rebirth in ways not anticipated by Chris Barnard's father, a "man of God". Some say that our tissues have become commodities, but this does not quite capture the matter. I would rather die than have a used car, but I am prepared to kill for a used kidney. Planned obsolescence, such a part of our modern lives, is not desirable in human organs.

9:

Even in the interests of self-justification, it is not my place to judge Chris's judgment. Rather, I have come to think of myself as the great man's archivist. Dr Watson provides something of a model: a sympathetic advocate who could document the hours of inquiry and innovation which went into every technical breakthrough. Somehow Watson managed to make us aware of Holmes's addiction to cocaine without diminishing the detective. Literature is full of such pairings, in which an ordinary man writes on behalf of another whose life is extraordinary but unreflexive.

My first encounter with the adventurous Sherlock Holmes was through a volume which Mother had borrowed from the mobile library for me during a particularly long season of distress. That's the kind of book that always has readers. As luck would have it, I began with a story that is little known, "The Adventure of the Norwood Builder". The plot involves the discovery of a bloody thumbprint.

While reading, I came upon a full inky fingerprint in the margin. Perhaps some innocent had been checking to see what the print in the story may have looked like. More probably, though, it was just an accident, the trace of a careless rather than a careful act. A reader writing notes, say, and copying out passages of the text had left an inky paw–mark on the corner of the page, betraying his journey.

"Look here!" I called to my brother. So delighted was I by the discovery of the mark that I exclaimed out loud. It occurred to me in that moment that Viv and I could compare our prints. He was making a model aeroplane at his small desk. The exciting smell of volatile glue comes back to me when I remember Viv standing beside me, peering over my shoulder. We had not shared much in the weeks since I had made my recent resolution to cajole him into giving me his kidney. My strategy at the time was to make him value me more by withholding myself, and so my outburst awakened him to our old bond. He pressed himself against my shoulder where I sat with my

Sherlock Holmes open on the desk. The renewed contact between us was a gift to him. I showed him the smudge and made my suggestion. Couldn't we use the small bottle of the red paint with which he was adding details to his little gun-metal grey plane, and compare our prints side by side?

"Look, you make your thumb print there. And I'll put mine next to it. Then we'll sign them and we'll always know whose is whose!"

The initial attempt was a smudgy mess, because of the viscosity of the paint. First his thumb, then mine. At a glance it seemed as if the impressions were identical, but Viv was more interested in detail than I ever was.

"Here. Clean your fingers properly." He passed me a small solvent-soaked cloth, and I wiped a red smear on to the grey square. "Now, try this."

He had a rather purple soft block in a little tin, a stamp pad of the kind that so intrigues youngsters. There was also a leather-bound notebook which had a spade and a diamond and a heart and a club etched into the cover. Only now do I realize that it was probably purloined from Mother's bridge club. Viv used it to keep a record of various moulded shapes: an embossed initial letter, or a coin surface. My mother's "Ex Libris" stamp was a favourite toy that recurred on several pages in the book, in various colours. The little image on the stamp was curious. An open book, with left- and right-hand pages reflecting each other, with her own name, Zoë, on the right and then written as inverted letters (almost a hieroglyph) on the opposite page.

Viv's collection of stamped impressions was extensive. Often a lustrous and thick hand-printed mark at the head of a page was succeeded by a column of increasingly fugitive traces which ultimately were scarcely visible except as damask ghosts.

Holding my thumb, Viv rolled it forcefully on the taut surface of the inkpad. Then with his hand laid over mine, he pressed my thumb on to a sheet of paper. The process was much like the one now familiar at US Immigration services. He followed with his own thumb.

Superficially you could see that the prints might have seemed the same. But there were the unique furrows, contour maps which suggested that he and I might well be following different paths. We were two unique continents. My blood thickened and slowed in my veins. Never had I felt so alone. Viv, however, was triumphant.

"See! That's you, and this is me." It seemed such an easy sentence for him to produce, but it launched me on a journey of discovery which was to inform much of my future.

10:

THE FINGERPRINTS TERRIFIED me. What were they saying about us? My brother's robust health always had seemed so arbitrarily his, while my own frailty was all too obviously a punishment. I was chosen to be the sickly one. There was no question about that, even though mother tried to discourage what she interpreted as a "morbid" tendency in me. Despite these obvious differences, I had clung to that word "identical".

How then, were we actually "identical"? I now understand that even though Viv and I have distinct fingerprints, our DNA is the same. That evening, however, the print confirmed my sense of myself as a fraud. Viv was more me than I could ever hope to be. Science explains it this way. In the case of identical twins, differences in the environments of the two embryos result in distinctions. The scientists stay away from metaphysics. They say that it is biology that gives rise to unique fingerprints. Each foetus receives information at imperceptibly different rates. A mother's body discriminates between the two identical beings. One will be first. That's the real meaning of separate development. Even though my DNA cannot tell that I have Viv's kidney inside me, my crime scenes are my own. Once when a youngster I soiled my shorts and I left them on the floor alongside Viv's bed. (Mother used to dress us alike before we went to school.) Somehow my trick was discovered and I was shamed not only with the act but also with the act of dissembling.

I couldn't understand who had betrayed me. Had I betrayed myself? As children we had often substituted for one another in simple pranks and we generally got away with it, using the easy dishonesty and mimicry that come naturally to a child.

Aside from my illness, the only exceptional circumstances in my life had arisen from that genetic accident of being a twin. A child longs for distinction; mine apparently was that I was not distinct. While I did realise how to exploit the advantages of being a double, I had a heightened need to be an individual. Before the onset of my kidney disease, I had outstripped my brother but by the time that I was about ten, it seemed I was lagging behind. I would lie in the dark watching Viv as he slept on the other side of our bedroom. Sometimes I loved and sometimes I hated him for looking so well.

While I shrank, Viv grew. I struggled to keep up when we walked on the beach. My eyes looked down at my feet to avoid noticing my brother's increasing stature. Then his shadow started to terrorise me as it towered over mine. Only after some months did I realise that I could manipulate my silhouette if I angled myself in relation to the source of light. Viv latched on to this, and he and I evolved a kind of lurching joust, in which each of us stooped and swerved like a pair of young albatrosses, competing in a landscape of illusions.

"Just playing," was the called response to my mother's rather fretful, "What are you boys up to?" as she heard us giggling, and slapping, and guffawing.

11:

AFTER A WHILE EVEN THIS game tired me out. Then it was that I became a long-distance reader. Francis Galton, Conan Doyle and Sherlock Holmes had all explored the significance of the fingerprint. The three men were contemporaries, and at times it is difficult to tell who has influenced whom. While Viv wandered abroad I stayed at home investigating these mysteries. I began studying identical twins and the puzzle of immunity. That inquiry became all-important once my condition was diagnosed. I realised that I would have to be self-reliant. Even Viv withdrew from me. Would my life become increasingly isolated? That shock I felt, but did not fully grasp at first. It made sense. Why develop an affection for someone who was about to die? Of course, it wasn't that straightforward. Viv's fear of loss had something of envy in it, too. Greedy for his mother's love, my brother began to mourn his own robust health. He became easy prey for me. I made Viv aware that if he was to donate a kidney to me there would be rewards. First, he and I would be able to go fishing together again; and second, he could become Mother's favourite. It was a modest case of domestic terrorism. I had become the intellectual one and so by reading him the story of Ronald Herrick, I could point out its significance.

"He was the first man *ever, ever, ever* to give a kidney to his twin."

While doing some investigating I accidentally came across the wrong Herrick. Robert, the cavalier poet, fantasises his own death as a bizarre act of erotic cannibalism.

Julia, when thy Herrick dies,
Close thou up thy poet's eyes;
And his last breath, let it be
Taken in by none but thee.

I play-acted the poem's morbid beauty for Viv. With a tightly-furled hand

I reached into my mouth, very gently drawing out my ghost while allowing my eyes to close. My taste for dressing up resulted in an impromptu costume drama and I draped my shoulders with a sheet. I was striving to attain the impact of Lazarus but suspect that I was diminished to a Halloween ghoul. With mock piety I reached over to Viv, and offered my pursed fingers to his lips almost as though I was giving him a wafer. Robert Herrick was taken in by Julia; Ronald Herrick was taken in by his brother Richard; Viv could be taken in by me. By willing my brother to imagine his kidney donation as necessary, I compelled him to sign a pact with me.

Since his death I have reassessed matters. At one time I felt guilty, because I used to think that he had saved my life at the price of his own. It recently occurred to me that this belied the case. I have saved him. Because of me, Viv lives on. Perhaps because of me Chris will live on, too, although it is possible that I have been taken in by him. This can happen to the biographer. It is one of the professional risks, as recent events in this country seem to suggest.

If I wanted Viv's kidney my parents had to commit themselves to the experiment. They must be my allies. Despite the urgency, I would have to proceed with caution. If I forced the matter I risked losing everyone's sympathy. I isolated myself from Viv, who needed to understand what it would mean to lose me. That was the most difficult of all. It was like betraying myself. Reading began to displace all other companionships.

12:

IN MY BEDROOM IS AN antique cupboard which has passed down from my great-grandfather. It is a tall elegant piece with a figured walnut veneer. The left-hand door is decorated with a fine curvilinear form, rather like a fan of seaweed, and the right-hand door is its mirror image. Whereas the motif on one door curls toward the left, the other symmetrically curls toward the right. This was a marvel to me as a child. How did the cabinet-maker find such a perfect mirroring in nature? Or was it, I fretted, an artifice, some trick to fool the eye? For months I furtively examined the panels in order to find where the cabinet-maker had spliced pieces together in constructing identical patterns. No such evidence existed.

Only much later did I learn the obvious: that the two doors did not echo each other due to some brilliant achievement at finding matching pieces of wood, or through cunning marquetry, as my childish self had imagined. Rather, the two doors were mirrors of each other because they were the same slice of wood, viewed as a recto and a verso set of pages. Laid open, the panels are doubles yet they are the same thing. Herein lies the enigma. Their identity is about to diverge. One millimetre from that plank of wood, the grain will tend toward difference. Just on the other side of the split the patterns diverge, belying the mirroring image of sameness that the two doors imply.

That was when I began to wonder about my brother. Had we arisen in this way, as inversions of one another, like an animated Rorschach test? We could not each be the hero of the same drama. Rather, we were antagonists. The initial occasion on which I voiced my suspicions aloud was when I spoke to Mother. It was already after dark. Dad was working overtime, and Mom was to meet him in the city for a late meal.

Every child has mixed feelings about such liaisons between their parents. Even though Effie was an adequate caretaker, these occasions always left me a little uneasy. Now, however, I remember the episode with a feeling of reassurance. It was still some years before my brother's death would lead to their separation.

I perched awkwardly on the end of my parents' bed, watching Mother as she sat before the mirror, applying her face powder. This was a marvellous ritual for me. First she would drape a flowered yellow scarf around her neck to protect her clothing, then she would pick up the pale moon-like circular box with her right hand, and transfer it to her left. Next with her right hand she grasped the lid of the box, which she would shuck slightly back and forth until the canister dropped slowly into her left palm. Finally, from out of that box she would retrieve a round powder puff of an indeterminate buff colour, which she beat very softly against the inside of the container, shaking loose any surplus powder. As I so often had, I watched her while she caressed the line of her jaw and the crest of her nose with the tablet of pale colour. The palette of her natural rouge blush tones was transformed into an even opalescent almond, through an alchemy.

"Mom," I said to her, affecting a rather careless tone. "I don't think Viv's quite like me." My attempt to woo my mother was a ghastly failure because she looked at me with her striking violet-coloured eyes and responded from out of the mirror,

"Yes, it's true, of course. But how long have you known?"

Those words were a betrayal. "Why didn't you tell me?" I accused her.

"We thought that you would grow to understand when you were old enough. We also didn't believe that it mattered very much."

What did she mean? What had I meant?

"We didn't want you worrying for nothing." She turned around on her chair and took my hand with a confiding gesture meant to win me over.

Instead of surrendering, as I so often did, I withdrew further. Who did she mean by "we"? Did the circle of conspirators include my brother? Was it my parents? Just my brother and my mother? I looked at the back of mother's hair, where the pins held up her French knot. My chest suddenly appeared in the mirror beside her face, as I rose to my feet. At the same time I made some feeble excuse about going to my room to listen to "Consider Your Verdict" on the wireless. I felt as if I was suffocating.

Something had been confirmed about Viv, and I didn't know what it was. Also, I felt as if the relationship of trust with my mother was broken. That is the case with secrets. They reveal the lines of affiliation. Who cares what a secret is? What matters, rather, is who knows it. I had spent my whole boyhood trying to identify whether there was any knowledge shared only between mother and me. Somehow it seemed as if Viv had always got there first.

Just some weeks before he died, he by chance revealed to me that his experience had been similar. It seemed as if Viv had always resented my illness because he perceived it to be the root cause of Mother's preferential regard for me.

My illness had always seemed the one point of difference between Viv and myself. I was the mirror-image of his easy self. Or rather, he was mine. Viv and Guy. Viv's small brown curl sprang from his left parting, just as my right parting arose from a lock of hair that naturally curled to the right.

I did not dare mention the incident to him. It was unbearable to imagine that he might laugh at me, or reject the idea. My research has taught me that even identical twins can be somewhat distinct from one another. That's a matter of timing, apparently.

Perhaps an identical twin lives too deeply inside a world of metaphors. So, for example, I could sit, on a winter's morning, with a blanket on my lap, watching my other robust self walk through the blue-kneed cold across the frosty grass on his way to the school bus. Blaming myself for my daily humiliations, I waited for him to return home from a day of history lessons, and debating societies, and cricket. My own experience was a pretty messy business, of doctor's visits, and blood-letting, dialysis, slow pain, and Mother's care.

My habit of reading "accident" as "design" has made me prone to conspiracy theories. My father had felt the need to repeatedly insist to me as a child,

"Coincidence is coincidental." That, of all things, is what I remember of him. It's a rather facetious comment to reiterate to a boy full of questions about the shape of meanings in the world, isn't it?

Some philosophers suggest that the preservation of weakness is the strength of our species. I am not in a position to argue this case. Perhaps it is as well that things turned out as they did. Viv and I were inevitably growing apart, just as the matching cupboard doors differ minimally and, despite the image of their sameness, are tending toward distinction. There is no explanation for why I was the damaged one. In fact I had been living via Viv for years. The surgery merely confirmed that fact to others.

13:

As USUAL, I DEFENDED myself through researching the question. Galton's ground-breaking paper in 1875 on the "History of Twins" was related to his work on fingerprints. His studies on eugenics no doubt developed in a dialogue with his more famous cousin, Charles Darwin. Galton's own scholarship became unusable because it was absorbed half a century later into a shameful period of unnatural selection. Stories of research using twins terrorised Viv and me. The devils filled our nightmares, though I don't recall who first alerted us to the grim history.

Still, as children we had undertaken some minor experiments of our own whenever we visited Uncle Enoch's farm in the Cedarberg mountains. You must remember that I led a somewhat constrained life, and these small pursuits served both to distract me and to engage Viv's interest sufficiently to keep him at my side, when he could so easily have skipped off to chase the rock hyraxes living in the hills behind the farmhouse. We two formed a kind of childish 'ethics committee' and together discussed what little surgeries we should or should not allow ourselves. Always imagining a threshold beyond which our research would not pass, we considered our pastimes innocent. As you might guess, there had developed between us an elaborate understanding of suffering through observing one another, and we variously resented, envied and pitied the frog on the cross.

Nature was far more delinquent than we were. She, it seems, is a relentless pioneer. The two-headed foetus of an otherwise perfect aborted lamb lying in the field beside an exquisite spring inflorescence of ixia blooms provided as much instruction on that score as I needed. A sport. Viv brought me a field trophy from a rock climb and presented it with a flourish. He stood on the lounge carpet with a wide grin, his hands clutched behind his back.

"Ta-da!"

The triumphant call produced a flourish of hands. On his left palm lay the feathered husk of an eaglet corpse, with its enormous bulging closed eyes staring at nothing from behind the taut skin of the eyelids. Then some months later he sings out to "come and have a look" at a *National Geographic* photo essay. He is lying on his belly in the living-room, the magazine open to a spread of images of brutal beauty. There, one eagle chick is about to boot its frail sibling-hatchling from the nest. The thin-necked one, marked for death, stares beseechingly up at the hook-nosed tyrant in the moment of fratricide. Viv, sprawling on the carpet beside me, says, "See that?" but the question is more of an assertion, and his hearty voice thuds against my ear like a stray cricket ball. I am acutely aware of his tanned and well-developed forearm alongside my pale and feeble limb.

Viv, by the way, made his own choice. A fifteen-year-old is a moral agent. My mother would never have decided for him. "Mother, if thou be willing, remove this cup from me: nevertheless not my will, but thine, be done." And in the case of a kidney, the risks are small.

14:

THERE WAS A TIME WHEN I resented that I had been held back a year because of my illness and what seemed to me a mercilessly slow recovery from the surgery. On reflection I can now see that this held the potential for me to become my own man, as it were. During this year my brother and I finally began to define ourselves as autonomous beings.

By the time we were ten the disparity in our sizes had become so marked that we exploited this difference. Two inches can mean a lot to a boy. As a family joke we developed a small performance that followed the conventions of ventriloquism. You know the kind of thing? A dummy sits on the actor's knee, ostensibly channelling his words. Though I was prepared to play the dummy, it was a kind of double bluff because I always spoke for myself, using a disguised voice. Viv had to perform as if I was following him, while all along he was following me. It must have had something of vengeance in it, and I remember the act empowering me to say one or two things which otherwise would never have escaped my lips. Ventriloquism has all but disappeared in favour of the less ambiguous muppetry-puppetry which is everywhere these days. As pure idea Viv and I are indistinguishable, but because we exist in matter, in our flesh, even our fingerprints have developed particular characteristics.

These events have taken on particular meaning because of Viv's Accident. When in his first year at varsity, Viv was involved in a commonplace car crash while out revelling with several new friends. Probably the vehicle was overloaded, and Viv somehow was flung against the gear stick. The new floral shirt which he was wearing was not enough to defend him, even though its exuberant playfulness had seemed to clothe him in immortality. That at least was what I thought to myself when I saw him preening in front of the mirror. Despite that shirt, a blow from the gear-knob ruptured his kidney. No one used seat-belts back then. Mom, Dad and I huddled in the hospital corridor waiting for an annunciation from expert opinion.

There was certainly enough blame to go around, and we all longed for some kind of miracle. The remarkable circumstance of Viv's situation couldn't have been anticipated by anyone and yet "Not Guilty" is a verdict parents don't easily apply to themselves.

Ironically Viv's premature death halted the process of my individuation from my brother. It ceased to be possible to tell which attributes I was developing that would not have been the same as my brother's. A gesture, a habit of mind: was that mine or his? I could no longer compare. As a result I have never forged a distinct character that was wholly myself. Neither did Viv.

With the passage of time, I have been obliged to concede that perhaps I have exaggerated the matter of our sizes. The difference, while so important to an ailing lad, may have been all but invisible to a casual observer. Acquaintances did after all struggle to differentiate between us. Even I at times am unsure whether a photograph captures Viv or me sitting on a bale of straw at Uncle Enoch's farm.

I look nothing like Chris, however. Happily I at last no longer have an exaggerated identification with him. Still, I am not sure that I know how to hold our stories apart. I cannot keep separate Chris's narrative, Viv's, my own, and the history of the transplant. They persistently become entangled with one another. From this period I have a scrapbook filled with cuttings and reports on various transplants. It dates back to shortly after Viv died, and it stands in as if it was a family photo album. Handsome images of the surgeon have in some ways become merged with my memories of Viv, all rigged out in his favourite blazer and slacks, on his way to the theatre with a gang of new friends he had met at varsity.

15:

[Here two pages have been pasted together. While it would be possible to separate them in order to recover what has been masked through that act, I am reluctant to tamper with the narrative as determined by the diarist himself. Once I let go of his intended design, there would cease to be any constraint on how I might order the pages. The result would simply represent the imposition of my will over his. Who then would be the author? – Ed.]

"Now you take care of that kidney," he once told me wanly as we lay side by side in twin beds during our convalescence. Then, "My kidney will be inside you for as long as you live." It was before daybreak, and the sunlight had not driven those cold grey shadows out of the corners of the room. It shocked me to hear the fact stated so bluntly. We had never really addressed the topic together before.

I felt as if he had punched me.

"What do you mean?" My question was pointless, and I stared at him.

"You know," he shrugged it off. Absolutely, I did know, although until that moment I had not fully understood the ramifications of his donation. A child can have information without being fully aware of the facts. I had been nurturing an immature notion that the kidney would be absorbed into my self, would become part of me. But no, it seemed. The kidney would always be Viv's.

That exchange altered much of my sense of being. Strangely, I recovered more quickly than Viv did, but then my life had only been enhanced by the operation; his had only been depleted.

In all likelihood Viv's comment was the origin of my need to seek advice from Chris, the great materialist. So it was that I was on hand to witness several of the profound effects of those historic times, and can offer an interpretation of the first transplant, an episode which had significance both for national and for international consciousness. The intellect can allow us both to evade and to pursue an emotional obsession.

The following narrative is composed out of various short papers and diary entries in which I documented the momentous years of the early heart transplants. There may be the occasional comment which now has a particular hue arising from the current mood in my country, but it is generally an accurate record of both a man and a technology. An "Apology", you might call it, but in the classical sense, not the rather self-serving duplicity that we have come to associate with "the apology" over the past decade.

Part Two

An Apology on Transplants

1:

"Now there's a man after my own heart!" – American newsman watching Barnard disembark from an aircraft

NO DOUBT, MY FEELINGS of guilt did not diminish with time. What seems likely is that they prompted me to contact Chris again. I genuinely did want to ask him about the Darvall family whose sacrifice was so absolute. That wasn't just a pretext. So it was that by the age of nineteen, I began to define my research interests.

Denise Darvall's fatal accident had made several of her organs available. Her heart went out to Washkansky, while her kidneys went to ten-year-old Jonathan van Wyk. I understand that the gift of a kidney is not total in the same way as the gift of the heart. But then, a heart is never given, it can only be taken. Poetry is a lie.

My scheduled first face-to-face interview with Chris was cancelled in what seemed to me a very cavalier manner.

". . . I have to prepare for a sudden departure," he muttered, together with a comment about a lecture tour abroad. "Couldn't we make do on the phone?" he asked. Clearly he had no recollection of our first conversation. What's more, he initially sounded irritable, as if he was just getting a task out of the way. Several rather evasive responses followed from both of us. I began to feel resentful. Offended by his offhand manner, I reminded him of our previous discussion. Reflecting back on my technique, I must admit that perhaps that was not helpful to me. Also, my questions were perhaps too personal and inappropriate. His relationship with journalists made them his allies as well as his enemies. All in all, he was wary. I tried another line of enquiry with more success. This was a series of professional queries about donors. Then he was immediately forthcoming.

"They are called good Samaritans. I don't have all that much to do with it. Bertie Bosman is the chap who takes care of that end of things."

In response to his comment about Bertie Bosman, I found myself thinking, "What does the phrase 'takes care of' suggest? What exactly *did* Bosman 'take care of'?" How did he encourage Edward Darvall to give over his rights to his daughter's still-beating heart?

Because I was reluctant to reveal the disparity in our ages, I did not ask Chris the right follow-up questions. I wanted to seem older, and so childishly I played at knowing more than I did. My telephone voice provided me with an adequate disguise. That silly vanity was an impediment to what could have been a frank and open discussion. My inadequacies prevented me from gaining some unique insights that would have stood me in good stead. At the time of that conversation many of the processes of the transplant team were something of an enigma. If I had been fearless I could have mapped an uncharted continent, but stupidly, instead of enquiring "Why?" I casually assented, "of course".

We learn these things too late, with the hindsight of maturity. It was only when he rang off that I realised what I should have discussed with him, although I didn't jot those thoughts down at the time, so am no longer sure what my insight was. There were so many unknowns that a more detached writer would have pursued. In the first year, apocryphal tales about Chris's surgical procedures abounded. Ghoulish legends of secret experiments circulated. All that we had to go on was the wild gossip that galloped up and down stairs like Dame Rumour. Dr Bill Hoffenberg, part of the Blaiberg transplant team, reported seeing a photograph of a two-headed dog which resulted from one of Chris's experiments. I cannot comment, because I have not seen it, but I do know that in the 1960s despite the politics of the day Chris twice visited Dr Demikhov in the Soviet Union. Demikhov had conducted just such an experiment and he coined the term "transplantology". Russia is now a two-headed dog that is devouring itself.

Once Chris's surgical processes were captured in print with the publication of *One Life,* his first autobiography, the mystery was translated into science. I was uneasy when it was initially published, fearing that it would displace my book, but ultimately I accepted that it was a resource rather than a threat. It was, after all, his story not mine. He told us more fully about the roles played by the various members of the team. That was the brilliance of their success, by the way. Chris established a group of outstanding medical personnel each of whom had a specific place within the complex organism that was the transplant unit. They were a theatre ensemble.

Let me try to restage that first transgression.

Mr Darvall has just lost his wife in the same car accident that has left his lovely girl unresponsive in the operating theatre. Someone says in a hushed tone that Denise is still alive. Cruel hope floods into the shattered man. Husband no more, he believes that he is still a father. Not so. At the end he holds on to her soul by giving away her heart.

Mr Darvall is persuaded that his daughter is no longer really present. "Brain death" even now is an unquiet idea. Would his decision even have been possible if Denise's mother had lived? Each parent would be grieving uniquely for the infant they had once received. Her mother feels the urgent surge to life as little Denise pushes from her loins; the exhausted father is overwhelmed at his first sight of the small swathed gift which his wife has given him. They each have given up some secret part of themselves in embracing their darling little girl.

It's hard to imagine how two parents could be persuaded, in that first-time-ever situation, and under such urgent circumstances to give up their daughter's heart. Neither of them could ever have considered it before, even as an abstract idea. It was not imaginable. Take out a beating human heart and stitch unto another! Unthinkable. So the fact of Mrs Darvall's death is probably a key element in what history had made necessary.

Although it is not quite the same circumstance, it is worth noting that my parents' marriage did not survive Viv's death.

"If you hadn't been so keen on the transplant idea. . . ."

"The op gave them both a chance. . . ."

"He was always your favourite . . . ."

Thus, my parents argue, but each time I play this out, it is a different voice speaking that last sentence, and it is never clear who was that "favourite". Through miming the hushed bickering which I assume must have taken place, I allowed first for one version, then another. There is comfort in ambiguity.

Surely, Mr Darvall's compliance at the hospital must have arisen in part from the reverence with which the medical community used once to be regarded? Back then, the doctor was someone who held your best interests above his own. We have travelled some distance since those days. It is a journey which Barnard himself navigated into a heart of ~~darkness~~.

Did Bosman suggest to the father that the sacrifice would give meaning to his daughter's death? Surely not. I now know from all that I have read that what Bosman achieved was to allow Mr Darvall to remember his daughter's own natural spirit of generosity. Bossie's talent with the families

49

of the terminal seemed to be his distinctive genius. While the surgical team moved themselves into a state of preparation, it would become a vital part of his role to quietly pass through into the room next door where the families of the grieving waited for some sign of hope.

"Yes, there is hope," he would explain time and again. "But it is hope for someone else's family. Would you consider. . . ?"

Several years after the death of Philip Blaiberg, Bossie Bosman committed suicide.

2:

'Dave . . . my mind is going . . . I can feel it . . . I can feel it.'
'I know that you and Frank were planning to disconnect me,
and I'm afraid that's something I cannot allow you to do.'

THE WORDS SPEAK OF fearful acts, yet there is no trace of fear in the voice itself. After telling us of its history, it goes on to sing.

Daisy, Daisy, give me your answer do.

Every year, religiously, since the revolution in home video in the late 1980s, I have watched *2001: A Space Odyssey,* on the anniversary of Denise Darvall's accident. The film is Stanley Kubrick's misunderstood film about brain death. It was released within a few months of the heart transplant, and I am always struck by what seems to me a clear coincidence of ideas. HAL is terminated by an impassive scientist who peers at us from behind a mask. How did Kubrick anticipate the journey which we were undertaking?

My family even now is unaware that while pursuing my research I had tried on three separate occasions without success to establish contact with Kubrick. In the early days, I wrote to him twice. Most recently I emailed him via his fan-mail service, although without much anticipation. Nothing. What I subsequently learned was that I had tried to mail the famous director on the very day that he died. There is no way of knowing for sure that this was not simply a coincidence of timing, although it did not feel as if it was. I had once (only once) written to Viv shortly after his death. By posting the letter to our home, I half-persuaded myself that he would be there to receive it. Prayer has had much the same success rate for me, and I have grown accustomed to the silence of deep space.

Even in the best circumstances fan-mail addresses serve primarily to block direct communication rather than to facilitate it. I felt vexed, excluded. We, the fans, are dangerous, and so must be diverted. That's the attitude. No special case is possible for me, the legitimate researcher. I am an irrelevance to the watchdogs until, say, I cross a threshold of legitimate research, and become a menace. Real alarms are triggered in virtual corridors. For example, an FBI profile is established for any scholar using the Internet to examine the psychology of the cannibal.

My questions to Kubrick were all relevant, although they could be interpreted as suggesting an over-determined set of preoccupations. The enquiry was substantially the same one I had posed to him after seeing *2001: A Space Odyssey* back in 1968.

"How closely did you follow the history of the first heart transplants? And who had been the adviser for the filming of HAL's demise?"

I was surprised that Kubrick never responded. Surely these questions interested him? While he was making the film he had followed every scientific adventure. The termination of HAL is surely his comment on the transplant industry. The film was released in the same year that the Harvard Medical School special sub-committee met to discuss the house rules by which to invent the legal category of "brain death". Heart transplants in the United States could not proceed legally without defining that idea.

In the closing act of *2001* we see the rebirth of Dave the space traveller as he passes through extreme old age. He lies decrepit and feeble on his death bed, and raising a hand he points up to a luminous bubble, or amniotic sac, or space capsule in which a foetus floats through space. Inside is a kind of star-child which we surely identify as Dave himself, reborn. Because of Western attitudes to reading, there has been a persistently literal interpretation of the film. Nonetheless that scene still strikes me as an apt metaphor for transplant surgery. Through organ donation we can live again. Ontogeny recapitulates phylogeny. My understanding may in some ways be coloured by Viv's kidney, but you would have to persuade me that there is another interpretation which makes sense of all of the details in the film.

The "Harvard Ad Hoc Committee to Examine the Definition of Brain Death" reinvented dying for the Americans in 1968. Their resolution states that "a patient is dead when the brain is dead, or when the patient has gone into irreversible coma". How do we know when the brain is dead? What exactly is an irreversible coma? If we know anything, we know that we do not know. Is it after seven weeks? Seven months? Seven years? Very few would wait seven years before removing the heart. The transplant surgeons were losing patience with losing patients.

3:

DID CHRIS EVER SEE Kubrick's film? It is of course now too late to ask him, and I regret that oversight. As it happens, 2001 was the actual year in which Barnard died, and he began his own space odyssey. It is more than likely that he had seen Kubrick's epic. It was screened at the Rosebank Cinerama in Cape Town in 1968. That's just down the road from Groote Schuur (Dutch for "the Great Barn"), the hospital where the first heart transplant took place. Kubrick's enigmatic film was one of the things *to do* that year, and Chris liked to do. I imagine that he invited one of the young theatre nurses, some leggy blonde persistence who wanted to be photographed with the glamour of Chris on her arm.

Kubrick made scientific thresholds into household commonplaces. Astronauts lying in pods like human pupae taught us about suspended animation, a technique that was vital for the success of the heart transplant. Early on, Chris's own experiments had placed the body in a kind of hibernation during surgery. Every idea has its own time. In January 1967 Dr James Bedford had become the first person to be preserved through being frozen. "Cryonics" it's called. At the end of 1967 Louis Washkansky's body had been cooled to allow for the passage of Denise Darvall's heart into his chest. Had this surgical research informed Kubrick while he was filming the human pupae? Perhaps the director had been introduced to Barnard's work at some point.

Whatever the case, it seems unlikely that we will honour our contract with the frozen cryonics pioneer. We are more interested in engineering woolly mammoths than in resuscitating an eccentric visionary.

When Kubrick's movie came out I felt an overwhelming need to discuss it with someone. Viv was already dead, and I hadn't yet forged any new friendships, so I was driven to turn to my mother, and took her to see a Saturday matinee. We had one of our rare arguments, because we somehow ended up discussing transplants.

53

"No-one is ever advised about all of the risks involved," Mother insisted. "Or they wouldn't have any donors."

"But if someone is actively dying, is the doctor bound to that life or to another who can be saved through a viable procedure?" I flung back at her.

"We are all actively dying all the time," she replied. I had no idea how dark her soul could be on occasion.

I think we were both disturbed at the termination of HAL. Brain death was a most astonishing description. Everything changed once that threshold had been crossed. Beating hearts cannot be ripped out of chests until the law says it's okay. We are so shocked that we call it 'harvesting'. What a way we have with words.

In the absence of other emotional climaxes, I periodically watch *2001*. There is comfort from the luxurious grief which it allows me, but that used to disturb mother. Rather like someone else's sex act, another's grieving strikes us as pornographic, disproportionate. At some point, someone feels the obligation to intervene and impose norms. Family friends make it an obligation.

"This obsession of yours is unhealthy. Your mother is worried about you. She's suffering too, you know." Thus, Uncle Enoch, who felt the obligation to intervene when I announced that I was going off to the cinema to see the film for the fourth time in one week. It is possible, however, that I was seeking some response.

"How dare you!" I shrieked in a voice of childish outrage. He looked at me with bewilderment. Was he too stupid to understand that I of all people knew how Mother felt after Viv's death? How it felt to let go of that other one in the room? His face had the look of crumpled idiocy which people get when rebuffed for trying to help. He had been slicing lemons and still had the small paring knife in his hand. With no intention whatsoever I clutched his hand, and the knife clattered onto the counter top. Snatching it up, I jabbed all of my strength into the wooden breadboard where several rings of pale cream fruit with citrus yellow rind lay in their shallow clear juice. The blade thrust its violence into the fine-fibred wood that squealed slightly in distress. Lemon juice, like serum, seemed to leach out of the gash I had made in the board. Uncle Enoch, aghast, fled from the kitchen.

My remorse was as sudden as my anger. I made my way out on to the veranda where Uncle Enoch was saving himself by pouring a gin and tonic. We stood side by side, each waiting for the other to apologise. After some minutes he pointed out to me that the lawn in the area of the pin-oak was beginning to turn brown. I noticed mother watching us from where she stood beside the apricot tree.

If Dad came back, would Viv?

If Viv came back, would Dad?

4:

THERE IS NO MENTION of Kubrick in Barnard's autobiographies. Still there is a brief narrative in Chris's *One Life* that will prompt any reader to think of Kubrick. It is the story of a young girl named Flavia. I was given a first-hand account of her when I interviewed one of the nurses who had worked with Chris. At that stage I was following all of the various threads that might give me insight into Chris's breakthrough research. Perhaps one of the nursing staff would disclose more than the surgeons who were his rivals.

Sister Myburgh (not her real name) had been on the ward when Chris took up a job at the Cape Town City Hospital for Infectious Diseases after returning to South Africa in the 1950s. That was almost two decades before the transplant. By the way, a common misperception is that the heart transplant was a sudden wonder. Actually, Chris had not won a sprint; rather, he had stayed the course in an endurance race. Or, if you prefer, decades of rehearsal led up to the great opening night.

By the time I interviewed Myburgh many years after the transplant, she was working at the Red Cross Children's Hospital. What I wanted to ask her was, "How was it, working with Barnard before his moment of triumph?" This, I hoped, would get at a real sense of the man. Just interviewing her made me feel his proximity. I also remember being particularly conscious that Viv was with me on this adventure. There always is some comfort in his invisible presence whenever I make my way into a new environment. It is so much more lively to have a companion. The forbidding situation of the hospital grounds hardly affected me.

Sister and I had arranged to meet in the lobby. It was the first true winter's night of the season. Several children with tubercular coughs lay on trolleys waiting for attention. One wretched little fellow whose face had obviously been melted in one of those ghastly shack-fires was running up and down the corridor pushing a wheel-chair and laughing out loud. The icy chill in the corridor and the slightly sour smell of disinfectant seeped into me. I simply have to recall that fragrance, and I am transported back to the encounter.

Rain, ceaseless rain, was driving against the building and the mountain was shrouded in dark forbidding cloud. Because I was lost in a reverie, I did not hear her approach. Of course, she was wearing those sensible shoes with soft rubber soles. In other circumstances I imagine the tap-tapping of her heels would announce her arrival. (I base this on nothing but her well-defined ankles.) Sister's stylishness was, even then, slightly out-dated. She had a cardigan over her shoulders and a watch pinned to her breast. You know the kind I mean, silvered with just a touch of marcasite ornament? She no doubt had been a striking beauty when a young woman, and was tall, with dark hair worn in what once would have been recognised as a Mary Quant bob. I was reminded of the "Eight Student Nurses" painted by Gerhard Richter.

The category "student nurse" even now seems to refer to a vulnerable individual. Sister Myburgh was herself perhaps "vulnerable" to Dr Barnard, as apparently many of her colleagues were. He was without question a forceful presence, overbearing. Perhaps some could defend themselves. There certainly were those who worked at the hospital in an outer circle, who were not within his thrall. Maybe these wary dissenters distrusted the cult. But a fellowship of true believers sustained the redemptive work through their commitment to his talent.

At my prompting, Sister reminisced nostalgically about those years. I pictured her solicitous compliance as she bent her keen intelligence to the will of the great man. She attentive, observing: he, fluctuating focus and abstracted absence. Chris would of course notice her compliance. These are lifelong habits.

In discussion with me, she did not deny *the surgeon*'s craving for celebrity, but neither did she diminish *the doctor*'s compassion for sick children. She recounted a brief anecdote to persuade me of Chris's attentiveness. That was unquestionably true, but it is also indisputable that he was attentive to her, too. Still, this story is not about Sister Myburgh, or Chris. It is, as I have said, about Flavia, one of a limitless pool of destitute youngsters with tubercular meningitis.

"A swollen football," was how Sister described the child's diseased head. I have an unhealthy interest in sickness, and so asked her for more detail.

"Nothing really could be done to help the wee mite." (Perhaps she had some Scottish ancestry buried inside her name. Almost everyone in Cape

Town has some Scottish in them.) "The infection produces an accumulation of fluid inside the skull. Her last weeks —"

Here she stopped and her gaze drifted away for several long seconds. Then she began again.

"Her last weeks. . . She spent her last weeks wriggling about like a worm. Unhappy, though. An unhappy worm, singing."

"Singing?" It struck me as unlikely. I had in mind the talking tapeworm which had driven Dimitri Tsafendis to assassinate Hendrik Frensch Verwoerd, the South African Prime Minister, in 1966. That was the year before the transplant. Verwoerd was Apartheid's Architect. It now seems unlikely, but he had been on the cover of *Time* magazine just a year before Chris was. They described him as a "brilliant diplomat and an inventive politician". Verwoerd, I mean. Perhaps they wrote the same thing about Chris.

"You say all she could do was sing?"

"Ja. 'Yankee-Doodle-Dandy.' That's all the language she had at the end. 'Yankee-Doodle. Yankee Doodle went to town.'"

The simple rhyme was all that had survived as a final trace of information. Inside my head I could hear HAL singing "Daisy, Daisy" in decelerating cycles of distorted sound. Art Imitates Death.

(Note to Self. Insert comment on GR's "Student Nurses": Richter's painting captures the eager sense of the trainee nurse as young professional. "Eight Student Nurses" for all the fresh energy of the women in the portraits, is an elegy to girlhood because it takes as its unlikely subject a group of nurses butchered in Chicago during a sadistic orgy by Richard Speck in 1966. Speck's grim slaughter prompted a kind of cultural outpouring and was documented not only in Richter's painting, but also on Simon and Garfunkel's *7 O' Clock News/Silent Night*. The Christmas carol incorporates the following spoken radio text, while Garfunkel's sweet voice carries the line of the Christmas carol "Silent Night":

In Chicago, Richard Speck, accused murderer of nine student nurses, was brought before a Grand Jury today for indictment. The nurses were found stabbed and strangled in their Chicago apartment.[*]

Viv gave me the LP *Parsley, Sage, Rosemary and Time* as a birthday present.

---

[*] Images of Gerhardt Richter's remarkable but chilling portraits of *Eight Student Nurses* can be viewed readily via "Google Images". That was where I found it when I was confirming that my recollection of the painting was accurate.

It was his first serious adolescent purchase, bought without Mother's advice. We played it endlessly to one another, singing selections back and forth in a cyclical duet, or a musical round. His was the radiant voice of Garfunkel. I sometimes hear my brother's voice singing, almost as if it arises from within me.

"Spek" is the Afrikaans word for "bacon". In America, "Speck" means something else. Mass murder is modern, and we were being left behind. How we have surged ahead since the end of Apartheid.)

[These notes Hawthorne has paper-clipped to his notes on a separate sheet annotated with the word "insert", which suggests that the information here was to be reworked rather than attached or deleted. I have retained this "Note to Self" more for what it reveals about the period, than what it says about the writer. – Ed.]

5:

IT IS IMPOSSIBLE THAT Chris's celebrity did not deform his personality. The operation was phenomenally successful, far exceeding anyone's ambitions, and the world watched hypnotised. You only have to look at the outpouring of awards from Princes and Popes to imagine his power. A Rasputin. It became all but impossible for me to get to see him. He was always in another city, another country.

There can be no doubt that in those early days Chris was aware that the transplants were transgressions. It was in defiance of convention that he had breached the norms about consent, mortality and morality, about care and decency. I wanted to ask him how he kept himself persuaded of the value of his project. Ultimately his strategy was to make something of a show of it all. Chris did not apologise – he and I are very different men. Still, his professional training was steeling him to make unsavoury choices. Closed off from any access to the voices of his inner world, he would do whatever was necessary. Through his intervention, the greatest mysteries became profoundly secular. Such a process has its costs. People who are less astute about these matters have described the heart transplant as a mechanical and technical event. Even Chris himself had gone on record paying lip-service to this opinion. "The heart is a pump." That was the assertion in his inaugural lecture. Obviously this is true at some level, yet I have never thought of the kidney as a metaphor for a dialysis machine.

Chris was born for the theatre, it seems, and at that inaugural he opened his talk in darkness with the sound of the heart's rhythmic lubdub thumping in the background. His hardened materialism in some ways arose from his hubris. He had become a broker in death. *The Lord giveth. The Lord taketh away. Blessed be the name of the Lord.* In saving one patient, he would have to sacrifice another. Homo economicus. Do the sums yourself.

6:

CHRIS BEGAN CHANGING HIS style, and we couldn't keep up. His were not the obvious needs of an ambitious Afrikaans boy from a mission household in the South African twentieth century. For some reason, he had chosen to be notorious, as if there was some achievement in that fact itself. There was only one world figure who had attained a similar secular adulation in modern history. I refer of course to Charles Lindbergh, the high-flyer who seemed at one time to define his century.

The house of history has many windows. I learned about Lindbergh, the first man to fly solo from New York to Paris, from my father. Nothing it seemed could tarnish his crown. Then his infant baby was abducted. Infamy pierced straight through his armour. We ceased to remember anything but that missing child. Just so, we now think of Chris as a lothario and not a transplant pioneer.

We no longer know that Chris was the first man to perform a kidney transplant in Africa; and we are also ignorant of Lindbergh's role in designing an early prototype of an artificial heart. Lindbergh, with Alexis Carrel, by 1935 had designed and perfected a "perfusion pump". This could keep organs outside the body supplied with blood and oxygen. What a threshold that represents. How do you understand an organ if you can only know it alive inside the body, or dead in a dish? Some have suggested that Carrel exaggerated the aviator's role in order to capitalise on Lindbergh's fame. Why would any man seek to identify himself unjustly with another's glory? Rather, the two men were collaborators, each in their own sphere.

Carrel was a collaborator under the Vichy. Lucky for him, shortly after the war he died from a heart attack, so the French never put him on trial. The "perfusion-pump collaborators" must have shared opinions. I can imagine the two men, in laborious hours in the laboratory, watching haemoglobin bubbling through a glass tube. There's not enough money for research, Carrel complains. There never is. Too little money going to too many people. The ambitious men share their opinions. The world's resources need to be redirected in order to maximise the talents of the talented. The times were too dangerous for either of them to be working with the enemy.

Can we divide this aspect of a man's career from that? Many people have often asked whether good medicine can come from a man with bad political judgment. Can good politics come from a man with bad medical judgment? This is a question which a biographer has to consider.

7:

I REGRET THAT I DID NOT know Chris before his great success. The person with whom I became friends was already by then a phenomenon. What was he like during the difficult years of ambitious endeavour, when he was still vulnerable? Periodic success there was, in those early days, long before he developed his interest in the heart. Yet certainly there were failures. How did he deal with those? There is something to be learned about how he coped with failure from his tyrannical drive to make his daughter into a world-class water-skier. Anything less than success, he derides. All or nothing, is his mantra.

Chris shows early on that he has the will to experiment with life. Such were the times. Surgical innovation is in the air. We all began to believe in it: anything is possible, so nothing is improper. One lonely evening in the animal lab at the hospital, he and his assistants surgically remove a litter from a pregnant bitch. They tie off a segment of the bowel of one little foetal pup. In the abstract, the violence of the event is unthinkable. The tiny warm, wet, living bundle is removed from its nest and an invisible hand mutilates it. Is there an end that can justify these means? Chris is able to believe so. That is part of why he is exceptional. The team is mimicking a deadly human disorder: infants born with a gap in the intestine, and Chris is developing a new technique.

He is edgy at work and at play. Feeling alternately moody and exhilarated, he anticipates the outcome. What will he discover? His result is awful. The bitch, on giving birth to the litter, eats her own damaged pup. Surely that would produce self-doubt in even the most ambitious of medical adventurers, and the tone of his record suggests that he is appalled. Still, it does not make him avert his eyes when he writes up the event.

"I could see her doing it: the tongue licking its offspring one by one until it felt one with black silk stitches. Sensing something was wrong, the mother had eaten it up." That is how he records the failure. He tries again, forcing the data to tell him something else. The Calvinist is methodical. He sets a watchman in the tower. Nothing will happen that is not observed. Immediately after this next trial, the puppy whose bowel has been tied off is discovered stillborn. This time there is a witness. That is the reprieve. *Ergo* the first puppy was not killed by the mother. It, too, must have been born dead.

"The puppy she ate was already dead!" Chris is overjoyed. Hallelujah! He has been forgiven. He whoops out in delight at the spectacle of the small black handful of fur. An abortion. That is of course what he needs to believe. Not infanticide, then! That is the most unthinkable of sins, even the rumour of which had tainted Lindbergh's life. The bitch's instinct to save the rest of her pups prompts her to remove the scent of death from the litter.

Chris makes us fall victim to the same error as he had himself. We are at first told that the bitch has eaten her damaged pup alive. He withholds what he had learned, so that we experience the full shock of his discovery. Yes, that is good storytelling, but it is perhaps something more. I feel manipulated.

Viv had made his own choice. A fifteen-year-old is a moral agent. Mother would never have decided for him.

8:

IMAGINE THE PSYCHOLOGICAL pressure of the early years of the heart transplant itself. Nothing takes place without witnesses. The news cameras from around the world click away during Louis Washkansky's final days. The patient's wife, drawn and grief-stricken, staggers into a waiting room. She wears a surgical mask which protects her husband from her. Despite all those years as man and wife, they were not, after all, one flesh. An observant journalist notes that her eyes are bleary, her skin is the texture of parchment. The photographers wait to capture her expression of fatigue. Will he pull through? they ask. Is their distress justified? they don't.

Louis would have died if Chris hadn't intervened. But still, it became inevitable that he died because Chris *had*. Washkansky's passing was a threshold event not only for himself, but also for every human being on the planet with access to a wireless. Millions living outside South Africa observed the events via television. Although we had proved that we were a modern country, Albert Hertzog, our Minister of Posts and Telegraphs, wouldn't let TV into the country. It was, the patriarch said, the greatest destroyer of family life in the West. So I had to wait, along with others of the South African general public, for the *SA Mirror* newsreel to show scenes that had already been screened to the world.

Days after the events we finally saw the crowds of reporters clustered around the entrance to Groote Schuur Hospital as a clutch of bewildered young surgeons stumbled out towards the world's gaze. That was in 1967. It was the year that the BBC had begun broadcasting in colour, but still, most who witnessed the events would have watched them in black–and–white. In those days you did not throw away a working TV set just because a new technology had come onto the market. Black–and–white still had its uses. Even now in South Africa after the end of Apartheid, we have discovered that black–and–white is not yet redundant.

Those of us following the Washkansky story woke from our dream of

65

global euphoria after eighteen optimistic days. The patient's lungs had become a patchwork of shadows from the infection which had begun colonising him. It was almost unbearable. My own immunological miracle, thanks to my brother, had removed me from the lot of common humanity, but still you can imagine how this story obsessed me.

I still remember the feel of my mother's hand on my face as she reassured me at bedtime, "You are my special boy." Despite everything, she was saying, my situation was one of extraordinary privilege. Once Washkansky began to lose his way, the common interpretation (still often repeated as fact) was that Louis had rejected Denise. It was an easy interpretation because men do that with girls that they have had. Actually, we were later informed that it was not the much-theorised rejection of the heart that killed him. Rather, it was the aggressive care which he was given. Huge doses of medications had undermined his body's defences against opportunistic infection. Washy's immune system had been suppressed. They irradiated him with a new device, the cobalt "bomb", and pneumonia exploded inside him. These things remain mysteries.

We all began to understand something about organ rejection. M.C. Botha was responsible for tissue typing. It was Botha who had declared that Denise and Louis were compatible. This was as close as she was ever going to get to any man. He developed a world-class lab that was in a relationship with Leiden. The Dutch had always been involved in the classification of types in our region.

Everyone had an interpretation after the operation. The procedure was a gift of God; it was diabolical; it was a scientific wonder; it was an ethical outrage. Shocked and distressed, Barnard could not comprehend the turn of events. He was losing not only the patient who until days earlier had shown every sign of the miracle. The phantom of his idealised self began to dematerialise, and failure rushed in upon him, as if it had been waiting behind the door all along.

Had his mother said to him, "You are my special boy"? That I cannot know. But I do know that the world media arrived in their hundreds to embrace the beautiful young man. 'What have you learned? When is the next?' It did not matter that after sixteen days Washkansky died. It did not matter because Chris and the news camera had found one another.

So the ambitious surgeon thrust himself onward, into the chest of Philip Blaiberg, who kept pace with his new heart for nineteen months, which was close to eighteen months beyond anyone's hopes. Blaiberg held on to life with a tenacity unexpected from his mild personality. Meanwhile

Christiaan oversaw his own Pilgrim's Progress. By the time I telephoned him, he had become all but infallible. That was how Chris bypassed the Slough of Despond.

Because Washy (as his friends had always called him) had survived less than three weeks, his rivals overseas latched on to this, regardless of other successes. The surgery was still too experimental; not enough was known about the risks; we had rushed into things. It has become a commonplace argument. Actually, the record suggests another truth.

The record, as it stands, tells us this: that four years before Barnard's success, back in 1964 the Americans, in the person of Dr James Hardy, had lost a donor just before the man's heart could be transferred to a waiting recipient. So in a desperate attempt to salvage something from the situation, Hardy stitched a chimp's heart into an adult human male. Imagine the surgeon's panic as he takes those faltering steps. On the threshold of a miracle, he finds himself inside a ghastly horror as he extracts the small beating heart from the torso of a furry primate who a week before had clung for affection to the arm of its caretaker. The corpse is left alone on the table with a hole in its chest, a familiar red cave that makes the ape look all the more human. The recipient died an hour after receiving the organ. They said that the primate's heart was too small for the human being. From what I have seen of primates and of humans, this is not a persuasive argument.

If the original donor hadn't died, the Americans might well have been the first. So actually it was accident and not probity that slowed them down. It was merely three days after Washkansky's surgery in Cape Town that there was another American attempt. This time the recipient was an eighteen-day-old infant. The donated heart came from an anencephalic baby. A young mother whose body was still flooded with the euphoria of giving birth had learnt that her infant has been born without a brain.

"Would she consider . . . ?" Nature is a shameless experimenter. So is Science. After the surgery, the tiny recipient died within six hours, due to massive trauma. Such were the gifts given on the path to redemption: the little one's heart might live on. A mother's motives are not the same as a surgeon's. Since then such procedures have become integral to medical practice.

On 2 January 1968, Barnard operated on Philip Blaiberg. He was our second. I was following the race when on the 6th of the same month Shumway performed the first adult human-to-human heart transplant in America. Shumway's recipient, Mike Kasperak, survived less than fifteen days.

It is as well to retain some scepticism about American complaints of the prematurity of Chris's experiments. They had been competing all along. Of course, when they lost they had to give themselves the moral high ground, but *they had been competing all along* and they lost. By the time that Shumway undertook that transplant between two adult humans, they had already tried with donations from a newborn infant as well as a chimp. I have frequently read that we are considered "cowboys" over here. Whenever I hear this, I remind myself that the real cowboys come from America.

All these years later I can admit that I had prayed for Shumway to fail. I didn't actively will Kasperak to die; rather I simply wanted Chris to outshine any star in the northern constellations. So while one heart recipient after another gave up in an American hospital and Blaiberg survived, I assumed that I had played a part in it all.

Let's be honest. Their objection wasn't actually that we rushed things. "Really, it's just that Chris is too damned successful," I explained to my mother. Blaiberg was the first heart transplant patient ever well enough to leave a hospital. O Lucky Man!

The best post-operative unit in the world: that was what Chris invented, and that was the secret of their success. They installed new sterile environments, kept the patient isolated (except for the occasional access to a news camera). Medicine had been lagging behind the surgical breakthroughs, because surgery was striding atop Chris's lean long legs, and it took medicine a while to catch up. By the early 1980s the techniques and technologies of transplantation had become routine. The surgical breakthrough had happened, but the unsolved challenge was how to deal with rejection. What was needed was the invention of a new world order. The pharmaceutical revolution was on its way.

"Rejection was something Chris had no talent for." A sour-faced nurse makes the snide joke in my hearing at a cocktail party.

In my own case the advances have been largely irrelevant. Viv and I did not know how to reject one another. An identical twin can receive a donated organ from its sibling without rejection problems. Still I remain fascinated by the research, and this is for several reasons. Insurance policies have taught us not to place all our eggs in one basket. Immunology might at some stage become a central concern for me, say if my brother's kidney inside me should ever fail. It is not impossible. I would then become like other men.

9:

Did Barnard steal Lower and Shumway's technique, as some have suggested? In the circumstances, theft is an impossible terrain for me to consider. Did I steal Viv's kidney?

The State of Virginia, 1972. Bruce Tucker, having swilled back several beers, stumbles against a concrete island on the forecourt of a petrol station. There happens to be no one to catch him and break his fall. That is all there is to a man's life. His head wallops against the solid kerb. Massive haemorrhaging and concussion are the results. Critical minutes pass by, as Bruce Tucker is rushed into the emergency ward, only just clinging to his tenuous life. A decision is taken that the man is "brain dead". Somewhere, in the same Virginia hospital system at that moment, a patient dying of heart disease lies in aching misery yet praying for a dark miracle. Is there a causal link between two sentences simply because they are placed side by side? Every attempt is made, they say, to find Bruce Tucker's family. Consent is never given, yet. . . .Yet Tucker's healthy heart is removed from his chest. It has become possible.

After the fact, Tucker's relatives set their hearts against the procedure. In the trial that follows, Judge Compton is initially predisposed to favour the usual 'legal' definition of death. Blood must stop coursing around the body; valves must cease to pulse; the body's organs, once flowing with vitality, should now like disused churches stand silent. The judge will not be persuaded that the extinct brain is evidence of death. What might it lead to? Who would be safe? The law would not hold.

Before you decry Judge Compton, note this. *He changed his mind.* Now that's a rare thing. Better a cautious judge who is open to persuasion than one reckless in the face of eternity. Compton finally rules that death might "in this case" be defined as the moment of irrecoverable loss of the functions of the brain. O wise and upright judge. A Daniel. And thus did brain death in the United States provide the definition of legal death, even to the fourth and fifth generation.

That judgment was everything. The heart transplant cannot even be considered without engaging with the complex metaphysical and philosophical question of personhood and consciousness. The Americans knew that.

In 1974 Andrew D. Lyons was on trial for shooting a man in the head. His lawyer, John Cruikshank, conducted the defence on behalf of his client. Cruikshank's ingenious argument was that the victim had died not as a result of the gun-shot, but rather because transplant surgeon Dr Norman Shumway had removed the man's heart once his brain had been defined as dead. Notwithstanding the inventiveness of Cruikshank's defence, because of Judge Compton Lyons got his share. He was found guilty of manslaughter. Dr Shumway was never charged, because brain death had already been invented. That was the effect of Judge Compton's ruling.

I have discussed this often with friends and colleagues. When do you cease to exist? Is it at the moment that your heart does not pump? Or are you no longer there only once your mind no longer knows that you are there? Kubrick's exploration of this theme has determined much of my thinking. What is the least part of you that still *is* you? Was the heart transplant bad medicine as some have claimed?"

[The question of theft interests the biographer perhaps above all other questions. – Ed.]

10:

IN THE MONTHS AFTER THE second transplant, much was made of a celebrated photograph. Blaiberg is seen lying at the edge of a wave which breaks playfully around him.

> [Without the detail which the following narrative provides, I would not have attached any significance to a rather banal photograph of a group of holidaymakers frolicking on the beach. The grainy image was so poor that I might have mistaken the image of a middle-aged swimmer for a picture of Guy Hawthorne himself. – Ed.]

The Associated Press picture shows youthful bodies at play around the man who lolls in the water. The photographer perhaps is suggesting that the youths' robust good health is a sign that Blaiberg is doing well. That image promoted the success of the heart transplant. "Look at the liberated man, look at his newfound freedom." This was of course some time after his highly publicised release from hospital. Dr Hoffenberg, who was part of the original transplant team, seems sceptical about that photo. "Just a publicity stunt" was Hoffenberg's feeling. Blaiberg was still profoundly ill. It is impossible to imagine that the heart recipient was not experiencing a great deal of discomfort, flopping around in the waves, even if the pain was masked by medications.

Dear Doctor: I do not sleep well at night. My feet are brutally cold no matter what I do; a bumped arm aches for several days; my food all tastes medicinal. I have strange weepy periods, when the slightest event will make me cry without inhibition. My hands tremble to such an extent that it is routinely impossible for me to write. I am terrified of every draught, and avoid human contact because I have become aware that most human beings pose a threat to me. I am prone to infection from the slightest cause. This is all despite the fact that I can, for the first time in years, walk without acute breathlessness.

Or some similar complaint.

In fact the whole episode became a political minefield, because Helen Suzman, the liberal MP for Houghton, was the accidental tourist who witnessed Blaiberg at the seaside. She came upon the melee of journalists, medical personnel and the patient while the scene was being set up on the beach. This is in Dr Hoffenberg's account. He had worked with Barnard, but I will return to his story later for what it suggests. Suzman observed that hospital aides, having carried Blaiberg to the water's edge, withdrew while the cameras clicked away. The fragile man flailed about briefly at the edge of the surf, before he was scooped up so that the waves did not overwhelm him. Do you know how cold that Atlantic ocean is? It amazes me that the shock didn't stop the old boy's new heart right there. That's not water to loll around in.

Hoffenberg has gone on record stating that Suzman was sceptical. A witness for the prosecution. There always had been a particular class of professional women who found Chris utterly resistible. (Professor Frances Ames, once head of neurology at the University of Cape Town, dismissed him as a talented delinquent. I cannot speak for *her* motives.)

In such a condition of distress, what would possess a man to venture into the surf? Did he merely capitulate to pressure, participating in a showy process that would drain his already depleted psychical and physical resources? A man as grateful as Blaiberg was could not resist being used. Chris had seduced him. I have some sense of what it means to be a bondsman to another. Is gratitude always mixed with resentment and a perpetual sense of having been manipulated? That's irrational, I know. We all owe our lives to others.

No doubt some measure of scepticism is warranted. There is some truth, some politics to any such account. There is certainly a dose of vanity, too. We all like to have been close to the epicentre of an event. We all like to have seen what others have failed to observe.

Maybe Blaiberg suspected that his own misery would be transformed if it was rendered useful to others. Pain is generally much less painful when it is experienced as useful. Perhaps, too, the ailing man had fallen in love with his surgeon? It may have been all or none of these things. Maybe he was being paid for the photo, and it was merely the banal financial remuneration that impelled him. A very, very sick man may indeed be grateful that his illness is of so interesting a type that he is able to sell it. That is easy to understand. He has developed a powerful regard for the quiet woman who does not mind getting up to call her husband's doctor at any hour day or night. Even before the surgery she routinely lowers him into the bath, and waits at the bath-side getting chilled because his floundering around has soaked her blouse. She sits on a low chair, ready to lift his unwieldy torso out of the tepid water. Given such circumstances, payment for the news story can serve as some kind of insurance policy. The Blaibergs did sell the rights of their story to the international media. How we hated them for it.

The record of that event is not so easy to interpret. I have scrutinised Barnard's own account of Blaiberg's recovery in his book *The Second Life*. Here he not surprisingly gives a completely different assessment of Blaiberg's resurrection after his release from hospital. We are told that the convalescent heart recipient was seen shortly after the surgery, visiting Rhodes Memorial on the slopes of Devil's Peak. Cecil John Rhodes was a transplant. Great bronze lions flank his Memorial and look down over the Cape Flats, more or less directly above the stretch of road where Denise Darvall was struck down by the car that mashed her brain with the shards of her own skull. The car-crash heard around the world.

It would be easy to dismiss Barnard's testimony were it not for the evidence in the case. As with the escapade on the beach, this simple adventure seems to have been observed, but this time by a witness for the defence. Richard Heald, a registrar from Guy's Hospital in London, was taking a break while attending the biennial conference of the Association of Surgeons being held at Groote Schuur Hospital. He happened to see Blaiberg clambering around the Monument. It is an unanticipated piece of good fortune that a young surgeon should happen to observe the world's longest-surviving heart patient wandering about with his minder, apparently at leisure. He scrutinised Blaiberg as they chatted. This encounter is on record because the young doctor subsequently wrote of it in the London *Times*. Heald's assessment was that Blaiberg appeared in general good health, and displayed no difficulty with breathing. The only evidence of frailty was a 'slight residual weakness of the legs'. What does that prove? You might say the same of me.

Of course the whole episode may have been staged. It is not impossible to imagine that Blaiberg was encouraged to visit the Memorial. It is not impossible to imagine that Heald was invited up the mountainside to the celebrated teahouse by a colleague from South Africa who was anxious about a threat to cut resources to the prestigious cardiac unit.

Cape Town City Zoo was in those days positioned just below Rhodes

Memorial. It is no longer there. Our zoos now look like wilderness areas rather than prisons. We don't like to think of chimpanzees in cages with electrodes like colourful liquorice laces dangling from their foreheads, and are uneasy with the claim that one human life is worth twenty baboons. Xeno-transplantation was Chris's dream, harvesting organs from different species at the abattoirs. The farm boy would solve the problem of supply using pork by-products.

Not everyone loves pigs. It has been easy to insult the swine who live alongside us. Familiarity breeds contempt. It also breeds antibodies. Pigs worked out how to reject us even before we rejected them. The surface of the pig's blood vessels is coated with a sugar that precipitates rapid rejection in humans. Our new strategy is to genetically modify the pigs. Dr David Cooper, a pioneer in the United States, had launched his career on Chris's coat-tails in South Africa. He edited a volume of reminiscences about Chris. Glamour by association, that's how celebrity produces value.

Mine was a different kind of attachment, born of love.

11:

CHRIS AND I DID NOT MEET for some ten years after the initial phone calls. This was an act of deliberate avoidance on my part. In that intervening time I resolved to follow his career at a distance. It was easy enough to do as he sought to keep himself visible through almost any means. By contrast I, as the exemplary invisible man, dread the day that I might become a figure of public notoriety, and God knows, I will neither court nor promote it.

The stations in Chris's history have become useful markers against which I chart my own life. It is somehow easier to remember what *he* was doing in the seventies than to recall where I was. After the death of my brother and mother I had to rely increasingly on aides-mémoire. An old iron box keeps together my degree certificates; close to one hundred photographs; two or three letters of particular significance to myself; the eleven postcards which I sent to my mother while on my first trip overseas. There is also a Marie biscuit which I kept as a memento mori. At the time I thought it a silly prank. I did not believe in death back then. That biscuit has become the object which I most value in the world. These bits and pieces now have a total emotional hold over me, but surprisingly they are of little use in prompting me to recall the precise historical context of the events which they summon. Recently they have struck me as unreliable. What has occurred to me is that these artefacts may in fact be fraudulent. Some of them possess no memory for me. Perhaps certain items have been added to the collection, assembled by Viv as an elaborate joke? His handwriting was pretty well indistinguishable from my own, especially to me. More than once he had falsely tried to persuade me that I was the one in some photograph or other. He never did concede those small physical singularities which I used as signs to distinguish between us.

Of course, Chris's life is a public record, and there is no possibility of its incidents being manipulated or recast. Through the process of reassessing his life and achievements, I realised, there existed a mechanism by which I might anchor my self. *He* lived inside history. If I could document his life, I would be in a position to locate myself in time. His first heart transplant was in the year that began with *Apollo 1* catching fire on the launch pad. A military Junta seized power in Greece, and the British Parliament decriminalized homosexuality, Che Guevara was executed, and the Six Day War redefined Israel's territories. That was the same year that Viv died.

So I began retracing Chris's footsteps, although my paces were considerably shorter than his. The career of the celebrity is marked by a random conjunction of likely and unlikely incident. It is always surprising, and yet predictable, to see what situations attract our current idols. It is extraordinary, yet not, to watch Barnard and his entourage stepping from a motor launch on to the jetty outside Albert Schweitzer's bush hospital at Lambaréné. He wears the easy glamour of the intrepid adventurer as he strides in uncrushed white linen through the mosquito-thick bush of tropical Africa. During those boycott years, he was our best export. So it is both striking and not so, to watch news footage of Chris being escorted between the little iron cots of the French military hospital in Libreville, where Biafran refugee children with doleful eyes stare up from a thicket of intravenous tubes. The beds in the images are from his description, pretty much the same as those which had contained the miserable little worlds of the children at the infectious diseases hospital in Cape Town where he had begun his career those years before. Perhaps we had donated those cots to Biafra? Biafra no longer exists. Do you remember it? It was a severed limb; and what had begun as a political ambition ended up as a by-word for human suffering.

My archive includes several remarkable yet commonplace pictures of Chris. Here he is with Peter Sellers opening a backgammon club in Johannesburg. The two men ape James Bond at the gaming table, while Sol Kerzner hovers in the background. The transplant surgeon necessarily is a high-stakes gambler. Sellers and Barnard are a matched pair. Humbert and Humbert. That was also a Kubrick movie. In the early days Sellers consulted Chris on the affairs of the heart, but the funny man turned his back after the surgeon's humiliation on the David Frost show. Barnard had been primed for prime time. Someone had given him information about a lawyer who was on the show to challenge him, although Chris had pretended ignorance.

By that stage of Chris's career his sexual indiscretions had become commonplace, more predictable than the roulette wheel, and so failed to hold any interest for me. The photograph now seems allegorical, a "wheel

76

of fortune". Back then, I was disappointed that Chris was so inelegant in decline. His fatal attraction to glamorous and ever-younger women is common knowledge. In this he was more ordinary than distinctive. So although it is diverting, it is curiously without significance to see him dancing with Princess Grace of Monaco, or lighting a cigarette for Sophia Loren. Sellers was devoted to the Italian beauty, by the way. There may have been more than one reason for the cooling of his bond with Chris. It cost Sellers his life, because he refused the offers of surgical help and died of heart failure.

"The King and Queen of Hearts." That's the caption to a picture of Chris sitting beside Princess Diana. Barnard is already a cadaver in that photo. Who could anticipate that he would go on to outlive the English beauty by four years? If you believed in witchcraft, you might read something into it: an old man eating a young woman. But you don't have to believe in witchcraft to understand that.

12:

IN 1977 I FINALLY SET up a meeting with Chris at the Harlequin coffee bar on Strand Street. The episode has a real significance because of the time we were able to spend alone in conversation. What has stayed with me is the emotional candour of the occasion. Little did I understand back then that this would be our last meeting. Chris's life became so international, and he was involved in various activities that necessarily left a modest local researcher behind. Still, I have relived the time we spent together because our discussion ranged so broadly, touching on so many topics that have come to have incalculable significance for me and for the country.

The Harlequin Café made real cappuccino back in the days when most South African coffee bars still served it with whipped cream. He was already seated by the time I arrived, and it was a real thrill to be able to walk directly up to his table to join him. You have no idea what an impact his presence had, wherever he was. Summoning up all of the personal authority I had, I approached him as if I had a right to do so.

He was very preoccupied, and nodded to me to sit down. Had he really remembered who I was from our very first encounter? There was some kind of misunderstanding, because he then asked me, "Which station did you say you came from?"

Initially I was quite touched, although a little puzzled. "How does he know I don't drive?" I asked myself. Mistakenly I thought he was worrying about my travelling by train on what was a typically miserable, wet Cape day: pedestrians up and down the street were being battered into lampposts as they wrestled with, or rather against, the batwings of inverted umbrellas. It was only as the conversation progressed that I began to understand how, because of the stress of his new celebrity, he had momentarily misplaced his recollections of me. The media were, after all, pursuing him everywhere. I saw his eye glance obliquely at my notebook. My strategic decision was to allow him to continue imagining that I was a journalist. Using a deliberate slow motion I removed my Parker ball-point pen from my inside pocket and ostentatiously flipped the pad open on its wire binding.

He spoke out immediately, including me in his world of ideas from the start.

"They are reeeally bloody ridiculous."

His agitated voice peaked into an unpleasant squeaky pitch flattening the diphthong into a characteristic South African long, high-pitched "ee" that somehow reminds me now of Mr Palazzotto's Neopolitan accent. He crossed his legs as he flung himself back in his chair. It was a single florid motion. I couldn't take my eyes off those hands of his.

"It's Sobukwe," he said with a measured carelessness that matched my own. He watched for my reaction, and the two words clearly were calculated. Like a tennis star, he calculated every serve in relation to the return. (Was he disappointed at my feeble response? The shot whipped past my ear and landed just inside the line. All that his comment called to mind was a photograph I had recently seen of penguins on Robben Island.)

"We've got Robert Sobukwe in the hospital," he followed up with a quick volley, having decided to ignore my indifferent return.

I began to take abbreviated notes. Barnard peered at the page.

"No shorthand?" he asked. His own long hands he splayed outward in the familiar gesture of a query.

"No – I – mm – I came to journalism late," was my inept alibi.

"Uh," he grunted, as he folded his arms across his chest, apparently mollified. "So, *ja*, I've got the old man in there, and he's recovering from a lung op. Already we've removed the one lung. *Maar dis nutteloos*. It's *hope*less." His voice swooped and turned mid-word. His right arm now flailed flamboyantly.

Chris was the older by two years, but he spoke of Sobukwe as his elder.

"Give him six months and the old boy's dead."

"Dead?" Shocking, that idea was. It was like a declaration of war. I have always had a limited apprehension of the political realities of my country, but somehow the word "dead", as Barnard framed it, filled me with unease. (I was going to say 'panic' but that would be inaccurate. At the time it still felt as if whites would be running the country forever. It always seemed to me as if we would pull through. Despite the volatility of the previous year, South Africa was on the up. Once law-and-order began to restore itself investment returns would soar.)

"I've had a look at his results and the X-rays," Chris continued. "You can just imagine that no matter how hopeless it is, we had to do something.

But he's a dead man. Out there" (he gestured wildly toward the street), "out there, they're so bloody stupid, I think they're pleased."

We both lapsed into silence. While I cannot say for certain what Chris was thinking, I myself was imagining what one might dread from the death of so significant a figure. When Sobukwe did indeed die in the following months, there was no bloodbath such as Barnard was implying.

Politics and medicine have learned this much from one another: engineered compliance can present itself as informed consent, at which point it becomes a great deal more usable. Viv had got entangled in this, too, and he ended up attached to monitors and tubes in a hospital-bed alongside mine. Staring at my brother when I began to recover, it was easy to think of him as my own much-manipulated, ailing self. I grieved for him who grieved for me. Thou shalt not commit transplant surgery. Had he really wanted to give me so much of his well-being? In one or two moments of delusion I dreamed of giving his kidney back to him. But then, in one particularly foul fantasy I dreamed of eating him in a steak and kidney pie.

After a few moments Chris continued. By now he was in the thrall of a cliché and I don't think he could really stop. His account summoned up a histrionic version of himself. Initially the other customers in the coffee shop were too embarrassed to watch and listen closely, so their eavesdropping confirmed what they had heard about him. I was aware of the averted eyes, the bashful feigned indifference. Much of what he said was in Afrikaans. I have taken the liberty of translating his words, though not his sentiments.

"They had two bloody security police watching over him in the ward. What did they think he could do? Here he is, a very sick old man. They've just removed a lung, but the bloody fool police have him under armed guard!"

He looked at my pad. I had stopped taking notes, but responded instinctively to the unspoken prompting of his glance, scratching indecipherable hieroglyphs on the page that could have been mistaken for a doctor's prescription.

"So I told them, 'Get out! Get out! This is a very sick man.' They just stared at me. 'You're upsetting him! OUT! Look, he's recovering from major surgery.'"

At this point in Chris's recreation of the scene, everyone was looking at us. The allure of fame is as literal as that. Candid staring replaces the furtive sidelong glances which acknowledge the rights to privacy of a normal citizen. A celebrity has no private life, and so our exchange was performed on a public stage. In such circumstances, an outside auditor is unable to recognise that what they are witnessing is a recreation of a scene from an imagined drama. Consequently I experienced the absolute shame of being bellowed at publicly by the man I most admired in the world. "He's not shouting at me," I wanted to say.

As he drew himself up into a pillar of fire, I was turned into salt. No use telling myself that he wasn't really shouting at me. We have all been instructed (in one way or another; by some authority or other) that an individual who has been abused is not actually the object of that abuse. Rather, the abuser is lost to reality, acting out a scene amongst the furniture of his or her own imagination. So I simply sat there passively, letting the storm exhaust itself on me. I have often subsequently thought of that day.

My anger and disappointment *now* are directed inward, rather than at external circumstance. It may sound hyperbolic to assert that I have never recovered my equilibrium. Why could I not defend myself? Chris was barely aware of what his behaviour might mean to anyone watching. There wasn't any intention to shame me. In itself that realisation was appalling. He just really had no idea who I was. There was no sense of our previous subtle conversations, no recognition of the months I had spent weighing and assaying his life in order to defend what at times might have seemed indefensible to an uninformed spectator.

Oblivious of my distress, Barnard derived consolation from the histrionic display. All the authority in the world seemed to gather itself into Chris's outburst, and he became even taller. My initial recollection was that he had risen to his feet as he bellowed, but this is unlikely. My memory of the volatile expression of wrath, however, is accurate. Of that I have no doubt. His reputation was all about wild tantrums at the hospital. Outbursts, one nurse said, that rained down on you and burned your flesh. Were those eruptions like this one, performances of authority? His command at Groote Schuur Hospital was based in his personal will, and must largely have arisen from the arbitrary exercise of power. Imagine what kind of person can dominate a phalanx of surgeons. An unreasonable demand can confirm supremacy more efficiently than a reasonable one. To yield to an unreasonable demand is to obey power.

By transferring my thoughts to the ailing Robert Sobukwe, I managed to escape that scene. I climbed into the hole in the famous patient's chest where that diseased lung had been. The great tree within the old man's torso had been struck in half. Could it possibly survive the storm? From where I sat inside him, the sawn-off branches seemed to be weeping blood.

My kidney ached as if longing for home.

While Sobukwe struggled to survive with only one lung, Chris was trying to craft for himself a complex persona as both public critic of, and covert apologist for, South Africa. I honestly cannot remember whether I knew this at the time of our meeting. In recent years we have learned of several notable South Africans who appear to have lost their way through attempting to play double roles. Barnard became embroiled in a misguided political intrigue with Eschel Rhoodie, a man so little remembered now that it seems unlikely that he threatened the overthrow of the nation only thirty years ago.

13:

ESCHEL RHOODIE. HOW extraordinary that what used to be a household name can mean nothing to the next generation of South Africans. Memory serves the present not the past, and no one can serve two masters. At one time Rhoodie was a government agent who precipitated a crisis that almost brought down the Afrikaner establishment. He had covertly been given administrative control over vast state defence funds. The revelations about this propaganda war apparently came as a surprise to many. So they said.

Rhoodie's role was to reward individuals who could help promote South Africa's image on the international scene. Few people were as international, few people were as seen, as Chris Barnard, and it was inevitable that a shell-man such as Rhoodie should have understood this. Here I don't mean to imply that Chris was not responsible for the alliances which he made. Presumably Eschel observed that Chris had already lost sight of the boundary between personal and political objectives. What was good for him was good for the country. It's an easy mistake to make. Chris was rewarded for defending the principles in which he did, after all, believe. An Afrikaner and a Nationalist: those were his loyalties. He did not consider that incompatible with his calling to be a man of the world. The Afrikaner was modernism, and the country's future, in his eyes. When Chris died, Mandela called him "one of our main achievements". Do you think that he did not know that Chris was also a damned fool, and a vain one? Rhoodie's disappearance from history is a good thing and it suggests just how far we have come. Now it seems clear that the private follies of a handful of apartheid apologists are no longer of any consequence. It is not the Afrikaner that places the country at risk. Rhoodie, by the way, died of a heart attack in Atlanta, Georgia, years ago.

Probably the illicit nature of the government agent was part of his appeal for Chris. At one and the same time he could enjoy the exhilaration of receiving covert funds, while thinking he was serving the country which he genuinely loved. The mid-1970s saw every adult male of a certain age and income imagining himself as 007. The role of publicity agent for the Apartheid regime clearly had some ideological appeal for Chris despite his youthful period of liberalism. By then he had rejected any communist sympathies he may once have flirted with. Much of the seduction, for Chris, was precisely that he *was* acting out a role, even if the character he was playing was himself. That's not so difficult to understand. He had all of the exhilaration of being a double agent while acting on his convictions. His marriage had been his training ground. Still, I am sure that while betraying one self he was being true to the other. The polygamist and the spy are basically the same type. Chris existed most fully at the point of intersection between the various versions of himself. This might even explain his convictions about the benefits of the transplant. His first autobiography, *One Life*, was followed by *Second Life*. The first book is the story of a man of science and is about the history of the Washkansky transplant. The other is largely a picaresque account of celebrity and the adventures of a lothario. It may be somewhat inflationary to view these, as I tend to do, as the two volumes of Faust's journey. Certainly, Barnard expected that his years of industry and intellectual investment would produce a substantial libidinal and financial reward. Certainly, there were those who had said, after the Washkansky op, that this man was in league with the Devil.

You can tell a lot from a photograph. Rhoodie has such personal attractions as would not have been lost on Barnard. The ladies' man often has a more fatal attraction to another man than to any one woman, apparently, as he is seduced by the irresistible emblem of what he himself longs to be.

As part of his own propaganda campaign Chris persuaded Channel One TV in France to allow him to do a special. He would demonstrate the complexity of South Africa's problems. Putting together the show, his first coup was to interview Breyten Breytenbach, an Afrikaner political exile poet living in Paris.

Chris tried to use Breytenbach's compliance to press Sobukwe to an interview. There was a cultural kinship between the two Afrikaners. Presumably that sympathy excludes the African. Sobukwe was more politically canny than the poet. He certainly had greater savvy than the surgeon, and his heart was unmoved, even though his lung had been. So Robert simply smiled mildly when Chris made his proposal. It was the politician who was the experienced operator. He nodded as if intrigued at Barnard's sketch of his ambitions for the TV show. Then he said no.

"He was just bloody well leading me on," Chris was emphatic. "Sitting there, smiling at me. Like he had all the cream. I told him that he was being stubborn. I told him, 'Men of vision like us have to act when opportunity presents itself. We have to make our own chances,' that's what I told him. Then as I was leaving his room, he nodded. I don't know why. He just nodded his head twice, like he was saying it was alright. 'Good luck,' he said to me. What did he mean, 'Good luck'? That was just too much. I asked him if he thought I was a bloody fool."

Chris's voice rose again as he recounted this final exchange.

He had so little sense of how bullying his persistence had been. It must have been some time since Chris himself had last dealt with rejection. Sobukwe's "no" meant that Chris became again that raw country youth whose genitals itched to be inserted into almost any one of the wild young girls with strong hands and weak wills who galloped around the hospital wearing crisp white uniforms.

14:

"Home is where the Heart is."

THOSE WORDS WERE PAINTED above an iconic bleeding heart on a wall in District Six. I thought of Denise Darvall's heart. In 1967 Louis Washkansky became her home. Was Barnard's surgical procedure a forced removal? Cloete Breytenbach photographed District Six, the heart of the old city that was ripped out by Apartheid legislation. He was Breyten's brother, and he had also photographed the *Time-Life* story covering the Washkansky op. Such coincidences would not be believed if you invented them.

Because in 1967 Christiaan was "the first", we mistook him for the *avant-garde*, the cutting edge. Barnard contributed to this impression. For one thing, he identified himself with the modern. For another, his personal vanity made him play at being years younger than he was. Anne Washkansky said that she was horrified (that is her word) when she first met Barnard. She thought, "This twenty-five year-old is going to operate on my husband." Of course, Chris was already in his mid-forties by then. So it was easy to overlook the fact that he had been born in 1922 in the farm district of Beaufort West, during a cataclysmic drought. A backwater without any water, as it were.

I have an early photograph of Barnard from a magazine. Above the image is a caption: "Girls, don't let him steal your heart!" This was where you can first notice the beginnings of a change in him. He no longer wears the ill-fitting and careless drab garments of the distracted country doctor. His long elegant body is very lightly dressed in a well-cut dark suit that looks foreign in fabric and design. Style is beginning to dominate over substance, as he shifts from doctor to celebrity. The opinions of strangers begin to matter more than those of his colleagues. *A Streetcar Named Desire*, yet more Vivien Leigh than Marlon Brando. Blanche duBois in a tuxedo, always depending on the kindness of strangers.

When I study that image I am reminded of how complex his relationship with his father must have been. Adam Barnard was a dirt-poor preacher in the Dutch Reformed Mission Church. A Smuts supporter in Hertzog country, with coloured parishioners. The poverty so bad that like frost it bites into you until the quick around your fingernails shrinks and your fingers start to bleed. When you've finished collecting frozen firewood you can't even feel your hands any more. So there's Chris, no shoes on, wearing shorts in winter until he looks like cruelty is his family name. And his father tells him, *Wees dankbaar.* Be grateful. Night upon night Chris watches his father in the old mission church in Beaufort West, thumping redemption out of the pulpit, while he, the son, pumps the bellows for the organ as his mother plays. Did this entanglement of mother and father, flesh and machine, ecstasy and obligation, suffering and salvation, instill his love affair with the heart?

And then here Chris was, all these decades later, coaxing us to believe that men and women can be reborn. It was after all a question of belief. Was he called to follow the doe-eyed man with long honey-coloured hair that, as a boy, he had seen in a friend's *Illustrated Bible*. The image was unlike anything he had seen at home, but he knew it at once. Christ holding his own bleeding heart like a breast-plate in front of his chest.

"Behold I stand at the door and knock." *Jesus Red*. Jesus Saves. So then, a Redeemer, not a Communist. The Afrikaans translation of the Bible was only published when he was eleven years old. *Die Bybel*. Dutch, it would have been before that.

"I saw the old man once," a hospital orderly told me in an interview. "His father, Adam. I saw him standing behind Prof. the whole time he was operating. Just think, there the father was, standing with his son while he operated."

In 1922 Adam Barnard named his son Christiaan. They were alternately, as their names suggest, from the Old and the New Testaments. For his followers, Chris was the new Adam, but he must defend himself against taking up his father's spiritual role. Once the TV cameras had discovered him, Chris decided never to allow himself to become another St Jerome sitting in the dusty desert beside his lion. Nonetheless they were both resurrection men, but each in his own way. Perhaps you have heard of the resurrection men? They were the body snatchers, grave robbers who disinterred human remains and sold them for use in anatomy lessons.

"Grave robbers! Cluck, cluck, how barbaric," we mutter at the very idea. But still, we would have gone to watch; we would have paid our twopence to catch a glimpse of the hanged murderer, with his skin peeled back from the navel to the chin. Was there something there, we might ask, within the sheath of the man's epidermis that could explain how the killer differed from ourselves? If you are looking for evidence of evil in the flesh, you will be disappointed. The corporeal speaks not of our difference but of our fundamental sameness.

This was something Barnard knew. Vel Schrire insisted that Chris had to get a white heart for Washkansky. Chris disagreed. For him, the only race that mattered was the one he had to win. The evidence is in the history. Chris mastered many of the new transplant techniques through doing renal surgeries. A kind of allegory works itself out through his first and only kidney transplant. The organs came from a coloured youth and Barnard stitched them into a Mrs Black who was white.

Don't misunderstand Schrire's position. He was arguing that with world attention focused on the cardiac team, it would not be possible to survive the political consequences if anyone started insinuating that at Groote Schuur they were killing blacks in order to give their organs to whites. Chris was already finding it increasingly difficult to locate suitable hearts. The neurosurgeons at Groote Schuur had grown sceptical, and were not informing him about possible donors.

– I don't trust him, they said publicly.

– I don't like him, they said privately.

They were envious of his celebrity, outraged by his promiscuity, angry at his power. If you reach the right decisions for the wrong reasons, is this the same as reaching the wrong decisions for the right reasons?

Despite the politics involved, by the time of our second transplant it was the heart of a coloured man, Clive Haupt, which kept thumping inside Philip Blaiberg for nineteen months. I don't know if you are sure where the human being is located. You might feel inclined to say that the body of a white man, Philip Blaiberg, was transplanted on to the heart of Clive Haupt.

Am I alive or is Viv? Is Viv alive now and not me? Perhaps he is. Perhaps I am. After my father left and my mother had died, who could have testified one way or the other which one of us had survived? There has been some comfort, I must admit, in being able to assert to myself that my brother's kidney is responsible for my occasionally lax habits, or my social failures, weaknesses I do not recall having had as a boy. Parents who adopt a child tend to blame their foundling's failings on the child's genes. It's Nature not

Nurture when the first act of delinquency takes place.

Given all of this, I am led to wonder whether Viv and I were destined to have such different futures. For now, all that I know is that I have given his organ a new lease on life, not just the other way round. Is it not Viv who should be grateful for the chance of an extended existence? No organ is an island.

Perhaps after all, if Viv had survived the car accident, he too would ultimately have succumbed to kidney failure. I was always the more precocious one and it is not impossible that we would both have ultimately "suffered" with kidneys, although as yet I have experienced no symptoms since the transplant to suggest that this is the case. The medical literature does point to a link between psychosis and kidney disease but this is so uncommon as to have little relevance.

Viv and I sit knee-to-knee in the bath. I don't even know which one of us has peed in the water. Do I end and begin at the surface of my skin? Disease passes without barriers between us. A person is a person because of other people. We die of one another. I am my brother's keeper.

15:

SEVERAL DOCTORS INSINUATED that Chris's tireless efforts to transform the racial politics of his operating theatre were really only motivated by self-interest. "He never did any more than that which served himself" is the line. This is an argument about motives, so I find it difficult to refute or to defend. What would *my* motives be? I have considered the case from a different angle by considering the two contraries of Accident and Policy.

On the Matter of Accident:

Denise Darvall and Louis Washkansky had no foreseeable shared destiny. Most likely, they would never have met socially. Perhaps they had once stood beside each other in line at Garlicks, while buying ties at the men's counter (she for her brother, he for himself); but such coincidence aside, their meeting was determined by no necessity other than blind chance. Absolute Accident is what united them. It is my sense that it would effectively have been impossible to anticipate the circumstance in which they were brought together into a single surgical environment. This was an eventuality for which no one could have planned. Certainly not Louis. How could a middle-aged man anticipate living a robust and whole life with a girl's heart inside him? No one had ever done it before. Remember, this was the 60s, and everyone understood that a man goes into a woman. A woman does not go into a man. Washkansky's willingness to embrace the idea indicates to me just how ill he was. That first surgery broke conventions and set up its own proprieties.

In all likelihood Washkansky was impotent. Erectile dysfunction is an indicator of heart disease. "Will I have to sit to pee?" he joked when told he would get a woman's heart. The ailing joker was reminding us that at present everything was in working order – perhaps he protested too much? Any medical symptoms associated with kidney disease generally disappear after a successful transplant, and no transplant is more successful than one between identical twin brothers.

On the Matter of Policy:

Let us now consider the situation at the hospital. The boundary between male and female bodies is surgically irrelevant in such cases, just as it is between races. In those days, just as there were male and female wards which would have separated Louis and Denise, there were separate sections for European and for Non-European patients which would have separated Philip Blaiberg and Clive Haupt. So when Haupt had a brain haemorrhage while at the beach, he was immediately transported to the ward for Non-European males at Groote Schuur Hospital. Through a statistically improbable chance, the mild-mannered dentist was at that instant lying in a ward for European males, feeling his life leaking out of him as he struggled against his failing heart. Of course, there was a chance that someone's heart would become available, but the chance that it would be Haupt is remote beyond calculation. No hospital bureaucrat could have hypothesised an Accident which might have united these two men through medical necessity. No apartheid administrator would have anticipated the matching of their tissue types. Planners are, invariably, deliberate beings. Policy is not the usual bedfellow of Chance.

It was only after another year of protracted dispute that Chris managed to persuade the hospital to set up a permanent non-racial intensive care unit for his heart transplant patients. This was at a time when banks and blood banks were racially separated.

It is easy for those who have done nothing to say that what was done was not enough. From what I read, I think Chris eventually achieved it simply because he was always absolutely bloody impossible until he got his own way. Under certain circumstances, that can be a virtue.

Picture two operating theatres. In one the donor moves from life to death, with a small specialist community poised like eager diners waiting for the carving to begin. In the sterile cell next door, the recipient is prepared for surgery. The pulse is slowed, incisions are made, and vital signs monitored. It is a moment of high drama. Hoffenberg examines Clive Haupt, the donor whose young wife has been encouraged to give him away. Time is suspended between breathing in and breathing out. With the transplant team waiting, their gloved hands point upward to the sky in imitation of prayer,

"For what we are about to receive,

May the Lord make us truly thankful."

The formulation perhaps has more charm in Afrikaans, as Chris would have phrased it throughout his boyhood. For him, the Lord is always Father.

91

Seën Vader wat ons eet,

Laat ons nimmer u vergeet.

No one moves. Hoffenberg announces that he can still detect neurological reflexes from Haupt.

"Bloody politics", at least one of his colleagues murmurs just audibly. Others shuffle with agitation, willing Hoffenberg to capitulate, because Haupt's heart incrementally degenerates as the moments pass. Hoffenberg is asking himself, "In what does Haupt's death consist, if his heart is pumping and his brain still clings to the world?" That is still unclear. It is not until the next morning that Hoffenberg concedes. The brain is dead. Surgeons move in, slice open the chest, extract the heart.

Dr Hoffenberg is part of a complex story. It was Hoffenberg who wrote about Barnard's experimental work with the two-headed dog. On the eve of the Blaiberg/Haupt transplant, Raymond Hoffenberg was seeing out his last twenty-four hours at the hospital because of a banning order due to come into effect against him the next day. And now here he was, being called upon to declare Haupt brain dead so that the young coloured man's beating heart could be extracted and placed into the chest of a white dentist. Don't let this pass by unnoticed. Barnard did not take charge of such decisions himself. Rather, he worked alongside a team of physicians who oversaw the interpretation of each moment of passage. Is that Caution? Cunning? Cowardice?

Dr Wada in Japan would learn that it is all of these. In 1968, it is a humid day on the volcanic Island of Hokkaido. A young man drowns while swimming offshore. Dr Wada declares the boy brain dead and transplants his heart. He suffers a sea-change/Into something rich and strange. At first Wada is a national hero. Then after twelve weeks the recipient dies, and a low murmur becomes an outcry. The boy wasn't dead, the transplant wasn't necessary. Wouldn't a valve replacement have sufficed, and where was the brain scan? Not murder, no. A double murder. Let us judge him, cast him out for his ambition. It took Wada six years of anxious litigation to climb out of the hole that he had dug in the youth's chest. Not for another fifteen years will the Japanese open their hearts to the procedure. The doctor has become a figure of mistrust. No one wants their captain to be a Shipman.

I hold no grudge against Dr Hoffenberg for his caution. Damned if he did, damned if he didn't.

"Haupt's brain shows signs of activity," he responds to quiet agitation from the team. The brain, it seems, sends out impulses. Is Haupt still in there? Everyone stands by and waited for silence.

Dr Hoffenberg is, after all, Witness for the Prosecution, and it is from him we know that there was no haste. They waited. And waited.

Was the heart transplant a South African story because we had no moral compass? That was Muggeridge's challenge to Chris on the BBC: you have a history of regarding people as utilities. At month-end I have occasionally found myself asking, "How is Mrs Peters useful to me?" My housekeeper and I have had brief encounters in which it has become evident that she is not unaware of the question, "How is Master Hawthorne useful to me?"

Barnard had not attended Washkansky's funeral. He was, however, present at Haupt's, where thousands of fans and supporters tried to touch the miracle-worker's jacket or his sleeve. A young woman claimed to have touched his heart. Did I mention earlier that I myself attended the event? The great surgeon's hands seemed sacred, like Christ's. To be touched was to be healed. Who, after all, could resist him?

As we gathered around the coffin, the silent body within the casket in front of us was not all there was. Although I am not a believer, in those hours I had a vision of the afterlife such as has not visited me since. I was aware that Clive Haupt's heart could be heard booming inside Philip's chest somewhere in the hospital up on the hill overlooking the graveyard. Is this all we need of hope? The king is dead. Long live the king. Vivat! Such a crowd there was at the funeral. Not until 1987 would I see anything like it. In that year, to appease an ache in my kidney, I went to Effie's funeral in order to bid farewell to the woman who had raised me as if I was her own. All along, it seemed, Effie had been a sympathiser of the political movement known as the PAC. This was a revelation to me. Robert Sobukwe, by the way, had been one of its founding geniuses. While for you that may seem an unlikely coincidence, Effie probably would have considered it a historical inevitability that a man who had played so major a role in this country should re-enter my narrative at some point. Barnard decreased so that Sobukwe might increase, but because of the ANC our story has now taken another shape.

16:

"WHERE THERE IS DEATH there is hope" – slogan on the office wall of transplant surgeon, Dr Norman Shumway.

The Swiss laboratory of Sandoz pharmaceuticals set up an initiative with its staff.

"When you next go on holiday abroad, just remember that you are a Sandoz employee even while away. Remember to collect a small sample of soil, place it in a secure sterile container which indicates where you found it. Then return it to us for analysis."

Of course, I have no idea of the actual content of what they said, but that was its substance. One such modest packaged corner of Norway contained an audacious fungus. Its properties are, I suspect, still inadequately understood. The sample promised a radical future for transplant surgery: it suppresses the human immune system. That's not what we are looking for these days.

What pattern of co-evolution between plant and animal had arrived at such an end? How did this vegetable menace arise? Why would a fungus seek to destroy me through undermining my own defences? Something of an amateur mycologist as a young man, I was always fascinated by the disguises and deceptions within the kingdom of the fungus. Perhaps my interest evolved out of the inevitable curiosity of the identical twin.

Viv was the dazzling toadstool, and I the modest mushroom. Despite popular understanding, some toadstools are edible, and many mushrooms toxic. The yellow chanterelle mushroom is delicious but must be gathered with caution because there are several noxious look-alikes. Nature has turned our appetite for novelty against us. The *Galerina* genus, the death cap, and Satan's boletus have all deceived the innocent harvester at one time or another. Who was mimicking whom?

"You and your damned experiments!" Mother had flung at me in a moment of vexed frustration. She of course regretted saying it immediately but I allowed it to hang in the air between us for several days. Blame is the raw material traded in family economies.

My mother in her declining years developed an obsession which she shared with all but the most remote of our visitors. She began almost everywhere to insinuate that my acute kidney failure had been the result of a childish experiment with a mushroom.

"Don't blame me or I'll blame you." I wanted to fling it at her like a handful of mud, but didn't. Still, we had several stinging disputes. Her argument depended on entirely circumstantial evidence. She insisted that my first symptoms appeared after I had tested a small sample of a novel fungus which popped up after a long period of rain. I, however, had been aware of the onset of the disease some time before my botanical experiment. Any child is reluctant to enter voluntarily into a relationship with a syringe, so I had hid my advancing illness. This she refused to concede. She accused me because she blamed herself. At the time I was so childish as to feel that she was blaming me.

I am still unable to enjoy even the common brown *crimini* (the portobello mushroom). It is no doubt due to my wholly superstitious aversion to tricks of similitude and word-play that I have avoided porcini ever since reading about porcine endogenous retroviruses. Those viruses, carried by pigs, cross species during transplants – and beyond, it seems fair to say based on recent experience.

Pharmaceutical companies hold us to ransom. We in return hold them in awe and contempt as we do God, and for much the same reasons. The promise of eternal life reminds us of inevitable death.

The wonder drug cyclosporine would change the whole arena. Chris could surge ahead. Then he retired from surgery. I refused to believe it.

"He's just sick of the media circus."

It was an easy excuse to deliver but in truth it misrepresented the case. Chris had not tired of the media. Rather, the media had tired of him. Drug companies were overthrowing the surgeons. The Health of Nations.

Who knows what Chris might have gone on to achieve with such an instrument. As a pioneer he was always aware of how he had changed the field for his successors. By the time that he wrote *The Second Life* in 1993, Chris could discuss the changed terrain. He had mastered the surgical technique; the problem of immunity was being addressed. The only lasting dilemma was the problem of supply. Even now, though, immunosuppression raises unforeseen problems.

I am in no position to argue that organ transplants have become too easy, but there is a danger if they become entirely routine. In the United States a cocaine user dies of a brain haemorrhage. Cause of death, presumed. No autopsy undertaken. The dead man's liver and kidneys were donated to three recipients. Within weeks all three had died of rabies. The donor lived near a cave. A caveat. Beware! Rabid bats!

In the first years after my own surgery, I developed the ungenerous habit of monitoring reports about the high rate of rejection amongst organ recipients. By measuring my health against the record of sickness in others who had undergone similar procedures, my body would be flooded with euphoria.

"What a distinction, to have received an organ from an identical twin." My ego defended me against being ordinary. That was the first thing. But there were also the medical implications, because in most cases the transplant patient lives forever on guard. What begins with the surgery ends as a lifelong battle to save the received organ from the body's natural immunological defences.

Often a second replacement operation may be required because the original donated organ is destroyed by the anti-rejection medications themselves. The citadel is besieged from within, and the last line of defence becomes the first line of assault. I had seen Civil War before.

You are divided against yourself. Burning tyre blockades send oily black smoke into the air; broken glass and razor wire line the streets, while a fourteen-year-old boy attaches a limpet mine to the wall of a schoolroom. A man is dragged behind a police-van along a gravel road until he gives up the names of his comrades, and even then his death is a slow and miserable business. An old woman struggling home with a month's groceries is attacked by zealous youths who force her to drink a bottle of cooking oil as punishment for breaking a boycott. At two in the morning a hut filled with sleeping women and children is wired shut and a burning brand is thrown onto the thatched roof. The police conspire with the murderers. We South Africans have been witness to such things. Just so the city of the self is compromised.

The human body will at times attack itself. My thinking on these matters has been directed by discussions about the viability of our new democracy. It is to the public good if we allow ourselves to reflect on our violent past. We are told that there is no other way to make sense of the present. While the patient does not always survive radical surgery, there often is no future without it.

17:

"Art imitates death."

In the mid-eighties I was contacted by Mr Palazzotto, a specialist dealer in medical *arcana* who had heard about my rather distinctive habits of collecting.

"I have some picture – special, special," he said in excited tones. "It has, I think, very interesting for you." The accent and idiom were regional Italian, perhaps originally from Trieste or somewhere on the eastern sea-board. He was in Cape Town visiting family, he explained, and had read a paper of mine.

"My shop, Professor Barnard he visit when he in Italia. He is saint. Reeeeally, saint." As Signor Palazzotto spoke, he tapped over his chest with his fingers pinched into a small knot. All of Italy, it seemed, had their hearts set on meeting the son of a Calvinist preacher who provided better guarantees of an afterlife than either Mary or the Pope. Through him they could be born again. "O lamb kidney of God that taketh away the sins of the world."

We arranged to meet at his hotel. I was tremendously excited, and couldn't wait to see what it was he had for sale. To my joy the print was laid on a small mahogany table right in the entrance hall where there was a corner of soft natural light. What Mr Palazzotto showed me was astonishing. It was an original etching (extremely unusual) of a *situs inversus*, a physical anomaly first identified by Marco Severino in the seventeenth century. *situs inversus* means "inverted position" or "switched around". In this rare congenital condition, the organs normally positioned on the left are, in one of a pair of twins, on the right hand. The illustration represented what struck me as the right-hand door of the wardrobe of my childish imagining. It was Viv's inner world become visible. The word made flesh, as it were.

The absolute position of the heart had always seemed a non-negotiable. One knew where the heart belonged with all of the clarity that, as a boy, I had understood why the servants' plates and cups were kept on the shelf under the sink next to the shoe polish and the Chemico. But Viv's heart was transposed, on the wrong side of his body. That is called *dextrocardia,* and it has afflicted both fictional and historical persons. (Donny Osmond and Dr No were both dextrocardias.) Viv and I were mirror images. No price would keep me from possessing Signor Palazzotto's print, but he struck a reasonable bargain in the end. Could an image of his organs compensate me for the loss of his dear self? For years I had been wandering in the wilderness alone.

The artist had decided that the limbs are redundant to the etching's purpose, which is to display the organs. Absent arms and legs seem to have been sawn off like logs, or like haunches of meat. They are not neatly sealed off in a sheath of skin, as in cases of *phocomelia,* the condition produced by medical science's experiment with thalidomide. (My generation remembers those days of medical audacity. Fertility drugs and the Pill competed for first position in the charts while we listened to LM Radio.) The cross-section of the remaining stump of leg as etched here is rather like the end of the half-leg of lamb which graced my dinner table last night.

Evident in the etching are the kidneys. They appear like two largish beans suspended end-on, alternate leaves on a twig. Of course, I had seen such illustrations before. You do not suffer as I had done without staring at images of the cause of your misery. As I left Signor Palazzotto's rather grim suite of rooms, I was aware of the aroma of cooking on the stairs, and imagined the kidneys on my father's breakfast plate beside two fried eggs with a link of pork sausage. Later as I made my way down toward the lobby I realised that the pungent smell was actually uric acid, the result of some drunken excess in the stairwell.

Part Three

The Anatomy Lesson

WHILE ASSEMBLING THESE documents I came across a short paper which I wrote several years ago as a kind of historical review or a cultural investigation. I have included it here for reasons which are rather opaque even to me. It is not by way of justification. It was not written by the man I am now; nonetheless it does demonstrate that I have over much of my life been engaged in a serious intellectual scrutiny which has guided my thinking and my actions.

> [These are Guy Hawthorne's own notes clarifying the status
> of the following essay. – Ed.]

"Doon the close and up the stair
Butt and ben wi Burke and Hare
Burke's the butcher, Hare's the thief
And Knox the boy who buys the beef!"

– from a Scottish popular rhyme

Western medicine has taken some five hundred years to make the passage from the first dissection to the first heart transplant. That path has several crossroads, or turnstiles, or gateways, all of which mark the various religious, legislative and cultural impediments to uninterrupted movement. I am, for my own reasons, more interested in those obstacles than in the open road. In other words, the obstacles to progress inform us of much more than that progress itself. Because the history of science is identified as a history of an ascent, it provides the exemplary narrative of the Enlightenment. Rash acts of intuition and transgression generally are read after the fact as faltering steps toward rational understanding.

As a result, anything which now strikes us as perverse or superstitious is not named within such an account.

The grotesque and spectacular appeal of public dissections throughout early modern history is explained as if our species was on an inevitable journey away from irrationality and toward the sun. But the truth is that only in fairly recent times has the anatomy theatre become the environment of the specialist with medical interests. Previously it provided spectacular public entertainment. Have you noticed the recent trend? It has become all but impossible to turn on the television without discovering a forensic show as part of the evening's programming. The genre has evidently displaced the detective thrillers of which I was always such a fan.

Several rather macabre plateaux mark the journey from superstition to science. Sometimes the archive has preserved a text, an object or an image which points to contradictory tensions within society, tensions which might make a sensitive imagination doubt that we have made any progress whatsoever. My impulse invariably was to discuss such enigmas with Viv, and as I matured I felt his absence most keenly. There was an incompleteness in me when I visited Europe for the first time on my own. He remained a kind of invisible interlocutor. Inevitably, as a South African scholar, one of my first pilgrimages was to the Netherlands, although my own parents were of English and French extraction. The Dutch had left so determining a mark upon the tip of the African continent that I felt I must explore those canals for myself. At the time I did not really grasp the significance of class in the various patterns of global colonisation, and so was astonished to discover the great sophistication and liberality that define the Dutch cities. This struck me as so different from my experience of illiberal Calvinism at the Cape.

At the Mauritshuis I saw Rembrandt's celebrated "Anatomy Lesson of Dr Nicholaes Tulp" in the flesh, so to speak. Do you know how it feels to encounter some great and famous work or other, having spent one's youth seeing images or reading about it from the isolated perspective of the colonial library? What I had not begun to apprehend was the meaning of the scale of a work of art. When I first saw the painting, I almost lost consciousness at the sight of that moonpale body laid before me, the doctor probing inside his arm. Like Freud fainting in front of Michelangelo's *Moses*.

Rembrandt's painting was not a harbinger of the new science as I had anticipated it would be. Yes, there is an indication of innovative surgical procedures and scientific interest, but the work was also brutal in a way which struck me as ancient. Perhaps I could rely on research to help me to an understanding of what it was that seemed much more foreign than familiar.

"The Anatomy Lesson" often is characterised as a group portrait, and it presents the likenesses of several important citizens of Amsterdam as if they are engaged intellectuals. From what I know of politicians, this is an unlikely claim. Portraiture is flattery by another means, and so the only hint which Rembrandt gives us that his sitters are not all scholars is through his handling of the various pairs of eyes. His figures all gaze in different directions. Curiosity and foreknowledge together lope around the operating theatre, exhibiting themselves to one another, sniffing each other's genitals like hyenas about to mate.

– *Did you know? Had you imagined? Could it be?* Some witnesses can bear to stare directly at the demonstration being undertaken, others look away. A few persons gaze out of the canvas at the viewer; another is lost in shocked abstraction. – *How did I get to be here?*

Only one or two are in the first instance interested in the dissection taking place. The man being laid open is a middle-aged Dutchman. That much seems evident. I have subsequently learned that he was one Adriaan Adriaanzoon, hanged for stealing a coat. At that time, in many European cities an executed thief could be buried in hallowed ground if the body had been given over for dissection.

These ostensibly are the first moments of the operation. A slicing into the skin and a peeling of the fruit. An unjust desert. The Dutch are good at the peeled fruit. Pomegranates, persimmons, peaches. But seldom the human arm. The learned doctor prises open the forearm to reveal *not seed and stone, but arteries, muscles and bone.*

All of this implies that the scene is painted from life. Is Witnessed. Despite the great attention to detail, both in the expressive features of the individuals and in the representation of that body itself, the painting cannot be the event as actually observed. The evidence for this is straightforward and archival because it seems that the standard procedure for such dissections was that the lesson began with the opening up of the lower cavity of the stomach and the removal of the viscera, in order to stop the rot. (No refrigeration facilities. Everything done in order to preserve the corpse in reasonable condition for as long as possible. Internal putrefaction undesirable; leaking undesirable.) "Anatomies" such as Dr Tulp's generally would be undertaken during winter for just this reason.

In Rembrandt's painting, while the arm has been dissected and is held up for scrutiny, the torso is intact. Are we watching, as some have suggested, an exercise in muscular manipulation? Is it "the body as machine"? Or could it be that Rembrandt is staging an examination of *the hand of the thief*? Perhaps he is positing that some aspect of the limb's criminality might be evident within the flesh? Is this Sharia'h law in the Dutchman's yard? What we see may be "evidence" of a proposition being tested by Dr Tulp himself. Begin with the arm because the doctor believes this to have been the locus of the Main Complaint. Maybe it is not Rembrandt but the good doctor who imagines that Adriaanzoon's proclivity for crime is physical rather than psychical or social. A magical mind might suspect that the thief is inclined to steal, and the artist must find a visual language, thus: "The thief has an ailing arm: the voyeur an evil eye." The doctor, sitting watching the unfolding drama of canvas and oil, urges Rembrandt on:
– *The hand. It is the arm and the hand that make the thief.*

Yet the body itself is intact. Anyone who has seen Rembrandt's ox knows that there is little about the inside of the body which this artist fears. There is nothing to stop him from painting the guts. In fact, he rather likes that slurry of mauve and puce with streaks of glistening white. Perhaps the painting tells us of neither Tulp not Rembrandt. It is invoking popular cultural prejudices, superstitious folly. *On one hand*, the painting indicates the future, yet at the same time is it not reminding us of Old Testament law? Poke out the eye that offends thee ("Susanna and the Elders").

Such sombre forces are not unknown even now. They can lead a man to poison a stand of water in an arid land, so that he might capture a vulture with an eight-foot wing-span in order to eat the discarded bird's eyes. The vulture is renowned for its vision, and so the great bird is butchered and its eyes eaten in order that the captor will be granted foresight enough to predict the football scores. *Swallows five, Vultures nil.*

The removal of the viscera. There is something dismissive in that collective noun, *viscera*. Kidneys, liver and spleen are all "lumped together" as one thing, a mess of blue-hued matter of unknowable significance. The internal organs and their vital role were for millennia almost wholly misunderstood. The livid purple sacks do not look like health to an untrained imagination; rather their opalescent lustre suggests toxicity. Bartolomeo Eustachi, sometime physician to the always learned Duke of Urbino in the sixteenth century, was the first person to write a treatise dedicated to the kidney, *De renibus*. His forty-seven brilliant anatomical illustrations include a drawing of the valve of the heart. Eustachi falls in love with the more modest mysteries of the body: the ear; the veins; the teeth; the kidney. He is married, as it were, to the Eustachian tube, to whom he gives his name, as is only proper. The Eustachian tube is the tiny canal which links the inner ear to the pharynx.

Meanwhile the great canal outside Rembrandt's studio trafficked scientific knowledge along the manufactured landscape of Amsterdam. A Golden Age. It was not until some two hundred years later that canals opened up the flow of trade between Edinburgh and Glasgow, precipitating a Scottish resuscitation.

By the 1820s, the Union Canal Company had begun drawing on a seemingly endless supply of unskilled workers pouring into the cities of Ireland and the Scottish Highlands at the end of the Napoleonic wars. A channel was dug using picks, wheelbarrows and human suffering. Miserable was the pay and the labour back-breaking. Two young men from Ulster, William Hare and William Burke (both presumably named for the Protestant victory), drifted to Edinburgh having heard that here, at least, there was work. Despite the layer of sweat that clung to his body and his clothes, despite his calloused and torn hands, and despite his surely broken teeth, Hare must have had some personal charms because he married the widow Margaret Laird, with whom he opened up a lodging house. All proceeded unremarkably until one November an impoverished army pensioner died in the room he was renting from Hare. It is difficult to dispose of a corpse. The body has substantial mass if left intact; substantial mess if dismembered. ("Yet who would have thought the old man had so much blood in him?" Perhaps they remembered the terrifying line from the Scottish play that cold evening in Edinburgh. Or perhaps they had never read Shakespeare.) The deceased had left little behind him. Pretty much the only item of value was his outstanding debt to his landlord, for a sum of £4. You know how these things go: in all likelihood it was money that Margaret and William, the property owners, had already spent. He nagged her or she badgered him. "Didn't I tell you last week. . . ?" To defray lost revenue, they decided on selling the old soldier's corpse to Dr Alexander Munro III, Professor of Anatomy, Edinburgh University.

Merchants generally have to take charge of delivering their merchandise; and even an old man is a considerable dead weight. Hare called on his friend and namesake, William Burke, to help with transporting the corpse. About to set out, the two men were advised by a medical student that a better price (per unit) could be obtained from Dr Robert Knox. An anatomist in private practice, at the height of his career, Knox was an apparently brilliant lecturer, and an impressive scholar. Twice President of the Royal Physical Society, he had published extensively in the *Edinburgh Medical Journal*. A surprisingly private man for one so public, Dr Knox had lived a rather reclusive life (perhaps something to do with the pockmarks which had left him severely scarred). Nonetheless, aspirant doctors streamed into his classroom to supplement the lacklustre university teaching they were officially receiving from Professor Munro, whose historical legacy leaves much to be desired. Charles Darwin's letters include a missive written home about Munro from Edinburgh in 1825, "I dislike him & his lectures so much that I cannot speak with decency about them. He is so dirty in person & actions." Thus Knox had over five hundred students in his anatomy class. Thus he was compelled to divide his students into three groups. Thus he was ever in need of corpses. Thus, thus, thus. Following circumstance only.

There is no evidence to suggest that, initially, Burke and Hare themselves did anything other than follow circumstance. The corpse had presented itself to them. We are an opportunistic species, and so once they realised the substantial rewards involved, they sought to establish themselves in what must have seemed a lucrative trade in a context where supply could not meet demand. Knox was willing to pay over £7 for a cadaver. Rivals in the procurement business, the anatomy schools were each only allocated one executed criminal per year. Legal constraint imposed a hypothetical limit on what was the burgeoning field of medical research. Circumstance *thus* had dictated that Edinburgh became the centre of an illicit trade, as corpses dodged their way from the grave to the lecture theatre. Several of the more substantial families fenced in their dead with a *mortsafe*. The iron cage wrapped its claws around and over the grave, assuring that there would be no resurrection of the flesh before the trumpet's last call. Hare and Burke were too entrepreneurial to allow such obstacles to impede their talent for commercial inventiveness. The men adopted an unconventional method for obtaining corpses. They became serial killers.

Apparently well-satisfied with the quality of the corpses he received, Dr Knox seems never actually to have met the two factors procuring his cadavers. The two rogues apparently dealt with his assistants, obliging fellows all, and it is unclear what the doctor did or did not know about the human traffic in which he was engaged. I have considered this question in the light of twentieth-century history, and it seems clear to me that a human being can exist within an epistemological twilight. "I did not know" has assumed the status of a quasi-legal defence, and we all understand what it means.

It has been estimated that Burke and Hare killed between thirteen and thirty luckless and homeless derelicts from the streets of Edinburgh. History has little information about the Mr and Mrs Gray who finally turned them in. The colourless couple had rented rooms in Hare's lodgings, and at some point they reported suspicious activities at the house. Things had gone bump in the night. These were curiously modern crimes, as far as I can determine, motivated by economic imperatives. None of the grand passion which seems to have driven Victorian Jack.

The Edinburgh police no doubt were a little sceptical when first alerted by the Grays. (I have no archival evidence of this, but I have read yesterday's newspaper, and that informs me about informants.) In this instance the police were wrong. Upon investigation, the body of a destitute Mrs Docherty was discovered under a straw mattress. Hare turned state's witness. State's witness did not turn a hair. Burke was hanged and Hare was saved.

Ironically, the executed man's body was given over for dissection to the incompetent Professor Munro (Alexander John III; Anatomy; Edinburgh) who had driven so many students to study at the private school of Dr Robert Knox. After the execution, a vengeful mob broke into the anatomy theatre while Professor Munro was in the process of removing Burke's skin from the body. In the midst of the ensuing scuffle, several sheets of this grim booty disappeared, and within weeks contemptuous souvenirs were hawked upon the streets of Edinburgh. Get your own piece of history. Burke's Best. Wallets and pocket books of original tanned hide. Soft as a baby's backside. Many museums today are squeamish about such relics. Still, the mind lingers over the unthinkable. Should you be interested, one of these grizzly artefacts is on display in the Anatomy Museum of the Royal College of Surgeons.

What of the brilliant anatomist, Knox? His legacy indicates that he was a personally vain and dismissive man, his moral sentiments perhaps driven out of him by the smallpox which had left him severely scarred and blind in one eye. "Dr Cyclops" some students called him. (We know how ruthless students can be.) Perhaps he could no longer identify with others. Still, a very snappy dresser, they say. Finest black bombazine, and a great jewel on his hand. One of the exceptional anatomical teachers of all time, he was hugely admired as a scholar, performer, linguist, translator. Destined, they said, to have had a significant impact on the next generation of surgeons. Knox's role in the business was subject to an investigation in which he was cleared of all wrongdoing, but he never recovered the stature which he once had had, and his value as an educator collapsed. What might his research have revealed if he had been allowed to continue without censure? He had published on the heart muscle, and there is no way of telling how his research may have advanced our understanding of that organ had the river of history not been diverted by the great Union Canal. Still, his role in surgical history cannot be ignored, even unto the fourth generation. In 1960 Edinburgh became the city to host the first kidney transplant undertaken in the United Kingdom. One Dr Michael Woodruff performed the surgery on identical twins.

Chris Barnard himself might have looked back along a chain of remarkable coincidence to Dr Knox, who, you may be interested to learn, had served for three years in South Africa, with the 72nd Highlanders.

Part Four

Plant

1:

I AM TOLD THAT IT IS unusual for a child to have a real sense of its own mortality. My brother, certainly, believed that he would live forever. Despite declining fertility rates we still seed our species from generation to generation, and guarantee our perpetuation. After Viv's accident, I began to understand the mystical force of the transplant. I had become Viv incarnate. The foetus is, after all, kidney-shaped. I was carrying his seed within me. These things are metaphors.

Viv's death certainly came as a surprise to him. An Alfa Spider swirling out of nowhere shrieked into the car bearing Viv and his companions home from the theatre. That Alfa was actually the cause of death, not the ruptured kidney listed on my brother's death certificate.

Both of Viv's kidneys knew the instant of the crash. The one inside me, even while I slept, was instantly struck with a bruising dark force which made my body ache for two days. I had never imagined what it may have meant for *those* twins to be separated. If you are sceptical, I have proof. When the hospital phoned my parents in the middle of the night I was already lying awake because I ached as if I had been lanced in the side.

Died of a broken kidney.

Arriving with my mother at the hospital, I was anxious because all of the grown-ups were whispering. I heard someone mention Viv's kidney. The word "rupture" was mentioned several times, and I could feel its potency. That diagnosis filled me with panic. Was I expected to give back the gift which he had given me? I watched Mother's face to see whether that thought occurred to her as she and I sat side by side in the waiting room.

Then, thank God. I heard a voice. It was the kidney.

"Don't give me up," it urged. Within moments of hearing that voice I understood that the kidney was now by rights mine. I was too young and afraid to examine my motives. My response was to avoid the matter.

With hindsight I began to understand my reactions intellectually. Now I understand that we cannot repay an obligation by giving back a gift we have been given. All of society would immediately collapse. To give back Viv's kidney would be ingratitude in the face of death – the idea smelled to heaven.

That was another interpretation.

Only recently have I been able to acknowledge the truth of the matter. As My Brother Lay Dying it never again occurred to me that he had a claim to his kidney. That is the real shame which I have kept hidden for thirty years.

For two days Mother and I sat side by side in the hospital. I kept on slumping like a child on to her lap. Of course I was a child, although I didn't know it then. A vast hollow opened up inside me, as I sailed off the edge of the known world. I could see the great jaws below gnashing as they waited for my little ship. Mother held my hand rather distractedly.

"For God's sake, Mom. Don't let him die." She turned vaguely in the direction of my voice but looked across the floor, beyond me, watching a movement across the grass outside of the waiting-room window.

When that letter from POST/OP arrived some eleven months ago, appealing for aid in soliciting kidney donors, it struck my adult self as an act of optimism and humanism to undertake or, rather, to commit myself or, rather, to resolve to help. I would be repaying a long-overdue debt. At last I could concede it.

The next six months I wasted trying to evaluate different ways of proceeding. I made out several little account books of various styles, in which I set out eccentric lists that tabulated my sense of what I owed and what I deserved, one moral lapse weighed against a quiet virtue. My impasse was only ended when I moved on to engage with the immediate question of logistics. How could I identify and secure the rights over an upcoming cadaver? That was a much more immediate dilemma. Possession is nine-tenths.

A first plan was to monitor the print media until the corpse of some individual voluntarily became available for harvesting. While I do recognise that a corpse is not in the position to volunteer, someone frequently does volunteer on its behalf. The Americans tell me that in the People's Republic of China, the state is willing to take on this role.

The difficulty when removing organs from the deceased is that timing is everything. Nonetheless, a real benefit of the cadaver over the live donor is that, with the case of kidneys, the ratio is two-for-one, because in many circumstances one dead body can be harvested for two kidneys. This is a one hundred percent advantage over the live donor where there can only be one kidney donated. The South African situation is at first glance decidedly advantageous in these terms, because we have no shortage of dead bodies. The problem is that for a kidney transplant, what is required is a healthy corpse.

Next it occurred to me that I might do volunteer work at an emergency ward. Through them I would come to know victims of violent assault or motor accident, rather than the diseased dead. This seemed a modest enough proposal. The added value of my scheme was that the bodies would be derived from a fairly representative cross-section of society. There would be a large, though not statistically unrepresentative, proportion of persons from socio-economically deprived backgrounds who had been preyed on within their own communities; there would also be a number from the middle classes who had been set upon while transferring their groceries to the boot of their car or in their own homes while preparing for bed. Also there would be the occasional industrialist or mining magnate gunned down by enemies (or friends). Road death, too, is no respecter of persons, and the donors would come from all classes, though this sample would possibly be skewed to favour the mini-bus taxi commuter.

Not long after, I began preparing myself for this through volunteer work "helping out" in the emergency ward waiting room. Soon enough, I was forced to admit that I was not attracted to the aesthetics of sudden death. My imagination *ran riot*, as they say. On going to sleep, I would see a knife sticking out of my forehead; my car window was smashed with a brick; I was bound to the kitchen table with the telephone cable; my dog was poisoned.

Abandoning the idea of the emergency ward as too overwhelming for one with my melancholy disposition, I turned my thoughts to the hospice. Perhaps I might quietly get acquainted with individuals stricken by some fatal but localised disease. In such cases, the continent of the self might have only one or two nations at war. (Happy continent!) Thus began one of the most intriguing periods of my mental life. Imagining my role as care-giver, I developed sympathetic relationships with people all over the city. How tender were my thoughts. As Saint Guy, I would visit the terminal with bowls of broth and fresh vegetables. A bachelor with emphysema, say, or a nine-year-old with cerebral meningitis. Periodic visits and a ministry of comfort would allow me to implant suggestions in frail hearts. Even the poorest among us might become a benefactor, I could suggest. With my hands folded on my lap to indicate that I was without appetite, I would sit at a bedside hinting of the immortality which was promised by organ donation. Through my ministry, grieving parents could be persuaded that a child would not have died in vain.

- You could end up inside a millionaire.
- Your recipient might go to Harvard, or
- His son could become an astronaut, or
- Her daughter the first female president of South Africa.

Clive Haupt in the chest of Philip Blaiberg. Viv inside of me. Parthenogenesis.

Sadly, that admirable scheme, too, had to be forsaken. Before it had even begun to take actual form, I became prey to a profound feeling of morbidity, which presented itself as a series of symptoms. I was afraid of pasteurised milk; I was afraid of unpasteurised milk; even bottled water tasted contaminated; my mobile phone-calls I restricted to emergency numbers only; and my microwave and television set became off-limits. In public places I wore gloves, and I gave up the daily pleasure of swimming in the public baths. Oh, the suffering and sickness within my city. My body began to send out new signals of its imminent demise. Small discomforts became warnings, and I lived an ever-diminished life. So ended plan two.

While recovering from this bout of melancholia, I searched everywhere for a sign. "Do unto others." The message was placed under my windscreen wiper.

Could I not perhaps identify a "living donor", an individual who voluntarily would give up a kidney through fellow-feeling? I could make available a range of informative pamphlets outlining the long-term misery of the sufferer. Here my own testimony could play a part.

Given the correct font and a sympathetic rhyming couplet, almost anything could be achieved.

A Special Bond with the Living
Is the Real Reward of Giving.

Why else have we evolved with two,
When only one will do?

Or, more simply, an invitation:

Read this testimony from one GRATEFUL RECIPIENT:
"We have been given two kidneys each precisely in order to test our obligation
to each other."

The Jesus Christians in Australia have a radical ministry of kidneys. For them, the practice of giving extends beyond the usual tokens. No donated old sweaters, ill-fitting jackets or used tennis shoes in their sentimental economy. Members are each encouraged to offer one of their kidneys for transplantation. It is generally ill advised to trust the individual who can persuade you to give away your own organs. But in all fairness I must concede that the leaders of the group themselves had led the way. They were both donors. Perhaps their sense of debt arose out of an anxiety about all those fellow Australians receiving kidney transplants in China.

The offering of a surplus kidney in order to save the life of another human being arises, I understood, from a moral equation. Yet how is a moral obligation transacted between strangers? Is it just an abstract quantity of sympathy that ties me to everyone in my species, even at a cost to myself? Any surgery carries risks and the recovery period is by no means pain-free. It still strikes me as remarkable that donation occurs anywhere other than at the graveside. The donor gains so small a compensation for the anxiety and pain experienced. Until recently the standard procedure entailed the removal of a rib. Tissue donation is as old as Adam and Eve.

Viv and I were both shocked at how long he took to recover from the surgery. One assumes that somehow the benevolence of an act will compensate for any personal discomfort or physical distress.

A wife feels cheated because the mystical nature of her gift does not assuage her pain after the operation. Some six weeks later she is surprised to discover that she still cannot without discomfort turn over in bed at night, and begins to resent her husband whenever he puts his new kidney at risk. How weak he seems if he has a glass of whiskey after work, thoughtless if he takes too much salt and pepper on his steak, or joins his office-mates in a game of soccer over the weekend. Understand, she has made herself vulnerable. She no longer has a back-up organ in the event of her own injury or serious infection. It is not that she begrudges her husband the kidney or his life of manifest wellness. Still, she cannot bear watching her organ being taken for granted.

The great lesson of human history is this: While your abundance should supplement my lack, you are not entitled to my surplus. Don't make the error of assuming that Viv's reactions are implied here. Never for one moment did he protest to anything but his own satisfaction at being able to help me.

The third alternative, something of a final solution in my own case, would be for me to donate a kidney myself. Although, of course, in my case, the grammar of that sentence masks a life-and-death slippage from the definite article "the", to an indefinite article "a". In my case, as I say, I have only *the* one kidney, and even that kidney is not absolutely my own. I really do not have a kidney to pass along. How different things might have been if I had received both of Viv's kidneys. That's what occurred to me. He died with a ruptured kidney within only a few years of donating his other one to me. "What a waste, as one kidney said to the other." Viv's joke.

If I had been given both of Viv's kidneys from the start I would now have that second kidney to pass on. There would then be no problem about finding a donor. I would be able to acquit myself of the great debt which I owe.

This is of course the deluded reasoning of a madman or one who is asleep. The logic evades me. By the way, for all that my thinking was absurd, there is an established practice of piggy-back surgery. It may sound bizarre from my description here, but actually it is far from an aberration. Current surgery often places a new kidney stitched into the body alongside the one that is ailing. The piggy-back heart was a procedure pioneered by Barnard. A polygamist, he never invested himself fully in one option when more were available.

2:

I NEVER DID RE-ESTABLISH contact with Chris after that brutal scene in the café. I couldn't help conflating our painful rupture with my father's abrupt and, as it seemed to me, histrionic departure seven days following Viv's death. Mom and I were both convinced that father regretted it, but that as a matter of principle he could not allow himself to come back to us. We were wrong in several interpretations. Really, I suspect that Mom and I both told this story because we were hiding our fear from one another.

In some ways I felt that Viv would somehow come back, too. Since those days I have accepted that it was not through a lack of will on his part. I must have confused Viv with Dad. Grief breeds delusion.

What occurred to me in a kind of redemptive insight only after a ten-year break between us was that I could possibly consult him about appropriate strategies for securing a kidney. Chris, that is, not my father. Perhaps Chris had colleagues within the surgical unit at the university who would be willing to assist as honest brokers in an arranged donation? That straightforward idea began to alter my dialogue with the world. The negative cast which had been colouring my furtive thoughts began to release me. With Chris's help I could re-enter society. I had been living as something of an outcast because of the strength of my imaginings. Given medical sanction, the "event" could become a "procedure".

I had just resolved to contact him when I was visited by the old dream. It was the dream in which I observe Barnard in his hotel room. The details are generally unvarying, but this time the dream was followed within two days by press announcements of his death. Some hints in those reports suggest that my vision (as I now call it) may have been a foreshadowing of objective fact.

The scene in the dream is so present, so immediate, that at times I can hear his thoughts. What I record here is not actually the dream, which is full of wild emotion and shock that I cannot explain. Rather, it is a waking man's record of his dream. I was awakened in a kind of suffocating panic, unable to breathe. Only years later did my therapist encourage me to keep a written record of my dreams in a systematic way. This 'night vision', shall we call it, was documented some time after the event, with as much precision as I could remember.

As always, it begins in Chris's hotel room.

He slowly unfolds the suit and the tissue paper, which are interleaved as if one thing. Wearing only a crisp white shirt, a dark tie and his underpants, he slips on the jacket to confirm the fit. He feels a slight anxiety that perhaps the shoulders are too narrow after all. About to drop his hands into the pockets in his occasional attitude of nonchalance, he discovers that those pockets are still sewn closed.

Scrabbling in his toiletries bag, he desperately looks for the small nail scissors he by habit always keeps with him. His fingers are awkward, fumble with unsatisfactory discomfort amongst the utilitarian bric-à-brac of a man's vanity inside the darkness of the cavity. Bits and pieces are in the way, as he tries to guess what it is that he is holding. It's wet. Something has leaked. He becomes aware of the pungent perfume of men's cologne. For the first time the combination of a clean masculine fragrance with spicy floral top notes make him feel nauseous. Worse, ludicrous. He feels ludicrous. Irritation comes to his help, and he plunges his hand at a small shape inside the bag, clutches at it. It's an overused travelling toothbrush. Why hang on to an old toothbrush? The flattened bristles are sordid, they have done too much service inside his mouth. Don't throw it away until you have replaced it, he repeats to himself once again. Positioning it on the bedside table, he now must remember to buy another. By involuntary reflex he breathes into his cupped left hand, inhales. His breath smells just slightly of death. He can detect those two cigarettes he had at lunch.

Still probing the contents of the bag with his right hand, he accidentally jabs his fingertip against the sharp nose of the scissors. Unsteadily he draws them from the dark green tartan pouch, almost spilling its contents. Reluctant to put the scissors down, he manages to draw his jacket off over his clenched fist. It is not easy. Like the monkey and the orange. The scent of some woman's orange blossom is in the back of his throat, and his tongue runs across his soft palate.

He does not remember them all. He tries to remember – any of them.

Flapping the jacket across his knees, he perches on the corner of the hotel bed. Unsteady even in the act of sitting, his long lean legs beat futilely against the air once or twice before he settles. Supporting his weight on an outstretched toe, he executes a balletic balancing act. He still has a swimmer's body. In the cupboard mirror, an aging Mastroianni (whose nose is disfigured by skin cancer) looks at him compassionately, watching the paltry struggle. With his slender fingers jammed inside the eyelet handles of the little scissors, he tries to compel the instrument to do his bidding. His hands cannot make the cutting motion with force enough to have effect. The little blades neither open nor close.

Giving in, he lunges with short sharp motions at the stitching along the edge of the pocket. A small dark rent appears in the beautiful Italian cloth. A little gash. His disappointment is the size of grief. His stiff hand pats awkwardly at the flaw which is barely visible, trying to undo what has been done. Finally the task is executed well enough to satisfy him, and he threads himself into the suit, slipping his key into the pocket. The exertion has distressed him and he finds difficulty breathing. It is with a sense of gratitude that he folds open the French doors, and steps out on to the veranda and into the cloying Cyprus night air.

I was not entirely surprised when I read of his death two days later. That is not to say that I was in any way prepared for it. How do we feel when the golden light that illuminates our days is removed from us, and the light turns back to a cold steel?

Initially the reports said that Chris had died of a heart attack. Actually he had asphyxiated from asthma. I have several copies of that newspaper report. I must have needed multiples in order to press the fact home.

So the tempestuous meeting between Chris and myself all those years before was to be our last face-to-face encounter. Our last heart-to-heart. That interview was the substance of what I now think of as our "friendship". Such things cannot always be measured in predictable ways. I ache with regret that I will never get the opportunity to explain to him that all of my most profound meditations on the human condition, as well as my most significant choices, resulted from his hold over my imagination. It is not a question of blame. Whatever I have done, I have had to trust my instincts. At the hour of my greatest need, Chris had withdrawn, much as my father had done years before. Nonetheless I did not feel any resentment over this, as it seemed to me that Chris, like Viv, had prepared me in order to undertake the last phase of my journey alone. At last I was by myself, liberated to make my own decisions.

119

3:

"HE'S GONE."

Father came and sat beside me. He could have no idea of how I felt, I who held Viv alive inside me. That fact was unchanged.

Viv had clung on for four days after the accident, drowning in the blood that seeped into him from his ruptured organs. When Dad told me the news, it was difficult to grasp that Viv was gone, because he wasn't. Not absolutely. I went to my room and looked into the mirror. Just for a moment I allowed myself to imagine: "If you didn't have that kidney inside you, you would be free of him." Then I thought, "If I didn't have his kidney inside me, I would be dead." In that moment, somehow what struck me with most force was the possibility of my own death, not his.

Trying to give the idea of Viv's death some substance, I tested the effect of the news on others. That afternoon I experimented on Effie. I heard her characteristic soft humming (some Protestant hymn or other) filter into the passage from the scullery and followed the sound of her to where a fragrance of fresh thyme and chopped onions hung in the kitchen. Effie was making her celebrated lamb stew. Buoyed by the familiar domesticity of the smell, I stood silently beside her for several minutes. An under-note of silver polish lingered in the kitchen, mingling with the warm aromas of the meal. I kept silent for several minutes. At last, in a voice that lacked certainty, I passed on the secret.

"He's gone."

She turned her head toward me, and I could see that she had already been crying for some time. "It's the onions," she said.

Three days later when I returned to school (remember, I was a year behind Viv because I had been held back) I used the simple line on two classmates. They were lounging together on a bench in the avenue of oaks, and were startled when I stepped out from between the trees. Repeating those two words in a lowered tone, I felt as if I was producing a properly

120

adult sentence to my peers.

"He's gone."

Their exchanged glances were startled, sympathetic and contemptuous. Did they even know what I meant? An urgent need overcame me to let everybody know what had happened. I wanted to blather childishly.

"Viv has died; he gave me his kidney to save my life, and now I have saved his because his kidney is inside me." Actually, I said none of it.

Walking away from what was becoming a small knot of boys under the tree, I felt the kidney shift slightly, a kitten stretching in its sleep.

Viv.

At times I have been overwhelmed by – what? A sense of abandonment. In your bleakest hours, you imagine that there will be no joy ever again. The earth will be consumed by fire. It will never stop raining. The war will continue forever. Then, suddenly, on rising one morning you discover that a migrating swallow has once again made its nest on the veranda. You notice, for the first time in oh so many months, the small pellets of mud streaking a careless pattern on the whitewashed wall, although those signs have no doubt been there for some days. Your piece of cheese with breakfast tastes particularly fragrant, and you can imagine the heavy-uddered cow standing in a field of sweet grasses. After which, despite the mundane and abstract quality of loneliness – its long greyness – instances of delight arise as rarities to be savoured.

There were the hallucinations that Viv really was still alive. Once or twice I dreamed that he was breaking himself off into small pieces and handing them to me like bloody petals. "Vivian Saves."

Dreams allow us to fulfil those wishes which we wish not to fulfil. In the dreams Viv's demeanour was calm and, may I say, blissful, almost sanctified. Those blessings were a great balm to me, as again my brother saved me from sure damnation. In one particularly memorable vision I saw myself standing in front of the executioner. Instead of issuing the order to "fire!" he took a small envelope out of his maroon breast-pocket. From that he extracted a letter of reprieve. As he opened it, the note unfurled like a flag. Who had signed it? I struggled to see, but the handwriting was illegible. Still, a voice declared that I had been forgiven, and suddenly someone was untying the bonds which held my hands behind my back. No forgiveness was possible . . . and yet it had arrived. Such things unseat a man's reason. Dostoyevsky and his companions were in front of the firing squad when the pardon came through. Sentenced to life, not death. They say that two of the men went mad.

Several of my friends have emigrated to the predictable places: Canada, the United States, Australia, New Zealand. There is nothing they can do to save themselves, as they splash in the shallow pool that they make together. From my experience, emigration defines one forever, like the absolute acts of murder, the sex-change or the transplant. Points of no return.

In some ways I did not really want to be forgiven. It would neutralise my life. That was the heart of the matter. Could it be that I was on a staircase which has only descending stairs?

4:

MY STRATEGY FOR DONATION had now been reduced to two possible solutions: either a dead or a living donor. The thought of using the deceased seemed to have arithmetical advantages. Two kidneys would be available instead of one. The other advantage was purely imaginary. In considering who might be a suitable donor, I spent some weeks in hallucinatory vengeance, murdering off my enemies. I spent days calculating whom I could dispose of, with least cost to myself. There was a substantial sentimental reward to be had from indulging my usual thoughts of homicide. Not that there is anything beyond the normal pathological in me. My murders are those of the everyday: mental acts of revenge against the malice, spite and petty lies of the workplace and the family.

I have ruled out my household staff in this calculation. Mrs Peters has been in my employment for over twenty years, and besides my understanding of her dependence upon me, I now find myself rather reliant upon her.

Mrs Peters replaced Effie, who had been knifed in the chest one month-end after collecting her pension. It was not until ten days later that news of Effie's murder reached us. More accurately, we were told of an unidentified body that turned out to be hers. I could not but think of her kidneys, by then quite useless.

Notwithstanding Mrs Peters's occasional tyrannical attitude to the domestic management, her disappearance now would make a significant difference to my life. No one else in my immediate acquaintance came to mind as a serious candidate. So I had to rule out the strategic neatness of accomplishing two objectives at once – the elimination of some particular enemy and the acquisition of a healthy kidney. The solution would have to be provided by an outsider. My final plan attained a poetic elegance. I would turn the tables on the opportunistic thief.

The strategy arose by chance. A pamphlet caught my eye. I had for some weeks been receiving flyers which indicated obliquely that what was needed to guarantee a break-in was for me to live in the most poorly defended home in the street. These leaflets were due to the good offices of a local security company. In an effort to boost sales, they have calculated what kind of information might instil panic in the general public. Thus the 'armed response' company is hoping to make us all sign up to grandiose plans for homeland security. The now-familiar calculation is that we will transfer our disposable income from securities to security.

"How to Secure Your Home" became for me a document on "How to Ensure a Break-in". I had been outstripped by all of my neighbours in the pursuit of household defence. Invasion of my property was inevitable.

Through taking no action, I had put myself into a situation which all but removed my control over events. I would be preyed upon. This they assured me. It was simple a question of timing. Now the legal argument shifted in my favour. This was my reasoning. Of late, several youths had begun to linger around my neighbourhood. If I allowed my defences to slip, one or other of them would inevitably force his way onto my property. It would be a question of self-defence.

My project to find a donor was never intended to become lethal to anyone. If it should, that would arise from accident rather than intention. No one can be held responsible for matters beyond their control.

Even for such a manoeuvre, planning is everything. I took the precaution of seeking the services of an expert, someone who would facilitate the donation of a kidney. What I wanted was an efficient surgical procedure that would leave the donor able-bodied and with every prospect of a swift and full recovery.

A voice inside me kept advising: "Don't get yourself caught up in long-term care." Perhaps that was Viv's kidney talking. Or I had begun to use the kidney as an alibi. Whoever it was, it persuaded me that I should secure the assistance of a doctor with considerable freelance experience. His fee was not insubstantial. That reassured me that I had no profit motive. My man was no longer employed by the health services, and sadly was prevented from formally pursuing the work for which he had studied so seriously for so many years. In our brief dealings, I found him to be perhaps more scrupulous and diligent than many others who are employed within the state hospitals. His bedside manner was exemplary and his personal style, combined with the fee, made me feel that I could absolutely trust him.

Some religions have a proscription on the trade in organs and body parts. Often donation is tolerated but not commercialisation. I don't hold with this argument. Between the doctor and myself there was a total commitment to the financial transaction, and that seemed not a bad thing. It was our point of honour.

I don't want to be misunderstood on this point. The settlement fee was determined by the marketplace. In the strictest sense, then, not criminal. Not even irrational.

"What is a fair price?" I asked him at our first meeting.

"We don't want to contribute to the violent crime rate in this country,' he responded. 'We would be paying the going rate."

That's a more apt phrase for the heart than the kidney. Necessarily, a heart must be paid for at the going rate. Still, I was gratified by the substance of his response. Was it possible, via the web, to determine the price of a human organ? Could I find the covert corridors through which the business of body trade was transacted?

How naïve. Any number of offers and invitations for body parts of various kinds are constantly available. The Internet is a boundless, bounding riot. Nothing within its reach is unthinkable because it is a universe without rule, or genre, or authenticating agent. Aside from the diet sites, there seems to be no superego, only id and ego. It has the limitless glory of the Inferno, and is wholly global. All things are possible. Film footage of Demikhov's two-headed dog is available on the Internet.

As a result of my investigations I became more rather than less uneasy about defining just what a "fair payment" for a kidney might be. A young woman from Sweden requires $250,000.00 for the organ while a youth from Mexico asks for a mere $15,000.00. These fees are payable to the donor, and the agent or factor is liable for expenses incurred, and will broker a deal that includes both costs and commission. Such expenses might include transporting the donors from their home country to an appropriate hospital with sophisticated medical services. Occasionally there are legal fees.

The recipient's task is to wait. They also serve. After the surgery, both giver and receiver are stabilised, and as a rule only the recipient will be given post-operative care. Perhaps the Swedish donor secures care as part of the contract. Generally, though, the follow-up treatment takes place once the patients have returned home, at which point their own economic circumstances certainly determine everything. I don't think that this sentence exaggerates the case. We are all aware of the inequities masked by the phrase "willing buyer, willing seller".

It is almost impossible to distinguish between actual practice and urban legend. A kidney is viable for an hour or so after death, and there is thus no real need for the donor to survive. If the transplant can be undertaken in circumstances which are less than ideal for the donor, the costs incurred are proportionately diminished. The websites are instructive. Invitations to prospective buyers explain, "have many Indian friends who are willing to donate. . ." or some such formula.

My habits of aggressive quietism allow me to overlook what I don't want to know. I act as if I have no agency, but I know this to be untrue; also, I act as if I have agency, although I know this to be untrue. Don't look to me for consistency. As recipient, I am both perpetrator and victim. My gratitude has made me ungrateful.

I imagine that I would be reluctantly willing, if my need were sufficient, to disable a man who is prepared to sell me his right knee-cap, if I pay what is for him the equivalent of five years' salary. I have already proven that I am willing to receive. Perhaps the cost to me was greater than the cost to my brother: he who was the donor. What is your own limit? I spend hours of my life gauging such calculations. One value after another is placed into the little brass pan; weights are reckoned; balances shift, and the scales saw back and forth like a child's toy. None of these dilemmas, I suspect, would have the same meaning for me, were it not for Viv and the gift of his kidney. Nothing can nullify my debt, nor quiet my expectations.

Having identified the appropriate surgeon, all that was wanting was a suitable donor. My man had taken the precaution to secure a place at a reliable clinic within easy distance of my home. That struck me as a good omen. Even though we would be dealing with strangers, there was something symbolically significant about keeping these events close to the immediate neighbourhood. It made me feel less vulnerable.

5:

PUTTING THE FIRST PHASE of my plan into action, I walk around the garden. The air is sweet and uncharacteristically still. What are the obvious ports of entry for anyone intent on housebreaking? I don't want to look as if I am inviting trouble, but neither do I want to appear impregnable. Are my vulnerable points sufficiently evident without being obvious? The bathroom window at the rear of the house, while itself elevated considerably from the ground, is rather close to the low wall of the outside laundry. The smallest amount of exertion can transform that window into an entrance. Further, since installing my burglar alarm, I have done a small-scale alteration which leaves the side of the house unprotected. The French door in the kitchen is a recent addition, and has not yet been connected to the security system. This is not visible from outside, but that does not mean that I am secure. The man who installed my alarm would trade such information as soon as the opportunity presented itself. Like any commodity, security data can be sold. There certainly are those who know the details of my house better than I do myself.

Our restless novelty in the matter of home defence always surprises foreign visitors to this country. Walls topped with electric fences are everywhere. So archaic is my own home defence that it is clear that my house is pregnable even to a minimally proficient burglar. Hopefully the property makes a more tantalising prospect than many of those on my street. My friends have often speculated on my apparent lack of security.

"He's depressed," they speculate. "That's the source of his apathy!"

The neighbours to the north have installed electronic beams which will detect any substantial movement across the full extent of their property. To their left, the Meyers were the first to erect electric fencing in our road. These technological adventurers have changed the tone of what, until recently, was a rather benign village. The residents feel that they will live forever. This offsets the dread that they are about to die.

By leaving my boundary largely undefended I have equipped myself for one of the most dramatic episodes of my life.

6:

IN THE MIDST OF ALL of these strategic plans, Viv's kidney made contact with me again. I am not a fool or a madman. However, as I sat in front of my computer the kidney asserted itself in a way that had never occurred before, nor has it since. I had heard it speak, but never before had I actually seen it. The organ projected a spectral image on to my computer screen. At first I thought it was just a reflected light from some source in the room. But as I stared at the soft snub-nosed crescent (which was rather like a segment of orange, suspended end-on), what became clear was that it was a vision. It was not self-evident whether that image arose from Viv's kidney or from my brain. Uncanny sightings have been reported, now and again, though always in remarkable circumstances and through gifted individuals, and rarely of bodily organs.

Matters of the spirit are entangled with the matter of the flesh. The encounter happened on what I have come to call "opening night", the evening someone finally broke into my house. Perhaps the vision simply arose out of my heightened condition. Was it encouraging me or warning me off? The vision of a kidney is hard to interpret. Its ways are unknown.

Seeing that image, I was somehow calmed. Viv was possibly trying to communicate directly with me as I ventured into what was becoming quite perilous terrain. The show was about to go on. Is that the right description? Not a show, perhaps, but rather a ritual, because everyone is a participant. No witnesses.

I am still wary of attributing a spiritual value to what transpired. Let me return to the metaphor of the theatre. It was, as I said, opening night. The back bathroom window was left ajar. The alarm was not set. The dog's basket was temporarily relocated to the garage.

But what if no one responded to my invitation?

– It's late. We wait.

– Will someone take the bait?

That was a small rhyme which Viv and I used to recite to each another when we went fishing together. My father had suggested the quiet activity as a sport in which my brother and I could engage together almost as equals. Writing this now, I remember us sitting on a riverbank. We are visiting Uncle Enoch's farm. It is in the old days when young white boys could wander off together to find frog, or bird's eggs. Viv is looking for red fin minnows because he has a crush on his biology teacher. I am just learning how to fish, and have thrown a line into the silver viscous surface. That fishing line threads Viv and me together, and then loops from our bodies into the rippling mirror where another pair of us sit on the bank of the river, somehow bound together with a fishing line. I hear Viv's voice chime beside me:

It's late. We wait.

Will someone take the bait?

7:

IDEALLY VIV SHOULD HAVE given an account of the proceeding events from her own perspective.

That sentence may not be *grammatically* impossible, yet it no doubt produces uncertainty for a reader with whom there is an implicit contract. Grammar is everything, and I have made it clear that Viv was my brother's name. Of course, art is rife with the tricks and enigmas generated by doubles. Strangely, even though a twin myself, I am never quite prepared for such encounters in real life. Particularly when these arise out of sheer accident, they generally have something of the contrived or engineered about them, so that it does not appear to happen as a matter of chance. There is something, dare I say it, *novelistic* about the fact that the individual who now has changed the course of my life was a young woman who had the same given name as my brother. Still, as I say, it would no doubt have been preferable for Viv to interpret events as she understood them. In the absence of that possibility, let me give an account of the events as I recollect them.

No one entered my property on that first night, nor for the three succeeding. I was full of expectant longing. Unrequited desire had reduced me to increasingly desperate measures. I unlocked the gate; I left off the yard light which illuminates the street and might have deterred a night prowler. Nothing. Don't let me create a false impression by implying that there is no housebreaking in my neighbourhood. Obviously, though, there was more to the whole system than I had imagined. Perhaps it depends on whether the moon is full or waning? I have heard differing opinions on whether this affects other predators, such as lions. For whatever reason, my home remained intact.

Several uneventful days. Then, at approximately two in the morning, overwhelmed with fatigue from anticipation and dread, a bizarre mood of rejection took hold of me. My eye stalked around the house. Here was any

131

number of desirables, surely? My B & O stereo-set; my notebook computer; several good suits. I could see that much of my money had been invested irrationally in books and music that would have no value for the petty thief; nonetheless, this surely could not result in the net denigration of my possessions *in toto*? My impressive collection of fine Zulu headrests may not be understood by the common burglar, but surely there was value in my iPod?

No doubt you want to know what labyrinth leads me to the she-Viv. It is after ten on the sixth evening, and I have just turned off the bath-tap in the main bathroom. I hear a soft slap. I subsequently realise that this is the sound of a magazine falling off the coffee-table in my living room. I am, as I have indicated, acutely aware of the sounds being made within my body, and so I at first wonder whether that lovely liquid, organic 'plash' is a sound coming from my involuntary actions. Then I hear a very subtle click, almost a nothing. The sound is somehow both familiar and foreign, but clearly it is not of the flesh. It takes me a minute or two to recognise the barely perceptibly "tuk". Someone has opened and shut my CD cabinet. Perhaps I should panic? Still, my thoughts are caught up with trying to identify what it is that I am hearing.

In a state of some excitement I almost dash downstairs, but a sudden thought stops me. How ridiculous is a man in his dressing gown! The flapping robe makes me almost wholly defenceless, girlish. Hastily, I drag on a pair of jeans and a T-shirt from the laundry hamper in my bathroom. In the planning phase of this break-in, it had never really occurred to me that I might come off the loser. For the past few years I have taken to carrying my father's old revolver around the house, and it follows me from room to room like a child. Though it has remained unloaded for over two decades, the gun still looks like authority. I snatch it from the shelf. On bare feet I softly tread toward the destiny that waits in my living room. A being crouches down in front of an open cabinet, its back toward me.

Possibly I transmit my fear chemically, but it is more likely that I make a small noise as I step on to the carpet. One way or another, some message travels to the creature before me, and with a burst of movement it leaps aside, turning in mid-air. Turning the tables, in fact. That sudden energy leaves me off-guard and vulnerable. I have lost control of the situation.

The face in front of mine contorts with defiant fury. It is snarling, in short guttural gasps through clenched teeth. Standing on my study carpet opposite me is a little thug, a force-field of belligerence. Still, it manages to be the object of my pity, my desire, my contempt, my wrath and my elation.

It's a girl, no more than sixteen, who challenges me. She is not just my thief, she is my guest. I, who have entrapped her, am both host and victim.

"SIT!" I instruct the girl. (It is not quite an invitation. Possibly it is a command. It is the same in English, which is how I utter it, as it is in Afrikaans, which is probably how she receives it.) She looks at me, momentarily assessing my authority. There is obviously something destabilising in the unfamiliar relationship of power between us. That instability impels her to comply. She begins to look rather miserable, as if suspecting the worst of me. An air of defeated listlessness enters her body.

Our situation is vile to me. I cannot allow her to sense my shock or she will gain the upper hand. The remnant of my authority is like the scrap of a torn flag, but it keeps her from assaulting me and plundering the house. We are at an impasse. I cannot continue to allow her to submit to me on these terms. Her compliance is, I know, temporary, and it has somehow made me ill at ease. We are seconds away from a transfer of power. I have established a bond between myself and a total stranger, a young woman as dangerous and as fragile as glass. I am now responsible for both of us. There is no way of anticipating how one reacts in such situations.

I address her.

"What do you think you are doing?"

"Your window was open," she responds as if that is explanation enough, which it is. Still, how could she know that? At which point she falters, her eyes flickering at the gun in my hand. I can see her heart beating in her throat. Ashamed of myself at being caught in so clichéd a role, I feel compelled to reintroduce civility into our exchange.

"I'm Guy," I say, feeling not disgraced, exactly, but certainly rather shabby, ashamed.

"I'm Viv," is her response.

Is she always to be better armed than I?

8:

FROM MY NARRATIVE YOU may have been able to detect that it is not in me to overlook offences or jests against my brother. My reaction is disproportionately defensive.

"What d'you think you mean by that? You're Viv?"

Though I can't imagine how it was possible, what occurs to me is that she may somehow know about my intentions. More than my home has been invaded.

"Sô waar. Ek's Viv. I doesn't mean nothing by it."

"Where'd you get that name?"

My words have an irrational intensity which weakens my position.

"From my Daddy."

She is too surprised to challenge my irrational query, but that doesn't stop her burbling. She has talked her way out of situations before.

"His name is Viv also, like after Viv Richards. That's *mos* a famous cricketer. Windies. Then my Mommy says she wants her first baby also to be Viv, only I was a girl, and they said it's okay because Viv is *mos* a girl's name."

Blah blah blah. She blathers on. Her uncle and her aunty and going to see cricket in Australia, and did I watch South Africa at Newlands?

I begin to feel nauseous. Why is she so at ease? Doesn't she understand her situation?

"Sit down!"

Nodding at a chrome-and-leather chair, I am pleased to remember that it invariably makes the sitter off-balance and uncomfortable. What is my plan? The fact of the matter is that I didn't have one. The scenes which had played themselves out as linguistic exercises in my mind have never anticipated this permutation of elements. Momentarily looking cowed, she follows my instruction. More calf than cow, with her long awkward shins and fragile ankles, she very awkwardly lowers herself on to the chair.

134

I nearly asserted that she "*reluctantly* follows my instruction". But on what grounds would I attribute feelings to her? Habits of language suggest that once a gun enters a room, everyone is acting under compulsion. Also that a young brown woman is in a relation of reluctance to an older white man. We read of such things. Actually, my sense is that a volatile and fluctuating dynamic passes between us. It is a flame jumping back and forth across a firebreak. At least one of us knows that the gun is unloaded. It is not reasonable to expect that she necessarily experiences these hours in the same way that I do.

I deliberately walk across her sightline holding the gun clearly in view, and sit behind her, where she has no idea of what I am doing, yet remaining aware of my presence. Some time to think. So it seems that the situation is new to me.

From where I position myself, I observe the line of Viv's neck, and the tendrils of soft hair just above her collar. (Her hair is bunched up in a ponytail.) Does her slight frame suggest illness, or is she in fact a lithe and healthy being? Does she take care of herself? Has she been taken care of? These are not disinterested questions.

"*Is she usable?*"

I am imagining her suitability for the proposal I am about to make. My research as well as my instincts has made it evident that I am looking for a homeless person from a good home.

A proposal. No. A proposition.

Too many meanings. I don't intend you to start imagining what kind of proposal arises in such circumstances. Don't allow your mind to linger over the length of her limbs, the width of her mouth, her high firm buttocks. Nor note that her warm olive skin smells slightly of coriander; don't consider the twin corridors into her. Don't notice such details. I do not. However, you might notice, as I do, the kitty charm which hangs on her low-slung belt like a bell-pull. A purple-stained love-bite cradles in the shadow of her collar bone.

Viv clears her throat nervously. There is a slight shudder in the back of her neck. Perhaps she is checking to see if I am still there, if I am still alive. Her thin shoulders and small back look forlorn, and I regret ignoring her, although I rather like that one-way communication. Then some remote instinct imposes itself. An obligation to be civil. How is that possible? From where I am sitting behind her, I speak.

I could have been addressing a stranger seated ahead of me on a plane in a sentence that is both neutral and sexual. ("Excuse me, miss, your inflatable cushion has fallen on to the floor in the aisle.") Actually, I find myself offering her money for her kidney.

She's a born negotiator. Within minutes it is clear that she has no qualms about setting the terms, and she demonstrates quite efficiently who is in charge. She knew someone who knew someone once who . . . . The bartering leaves me strangely tired, while Viv seems energised by it. There must be more trade in her background than in mine.

My opinion has always been that the state has no role in the private contract. Which does not mean that I have no regard for economic regulation. Generally speaking, I support the right to strike. We are being educated about such matters in this country. But it seems to me that certain spheres of voluntary economic activity are beyond the purposes of the state. Still, even I was astonished by an event of a culinary nature which recently arose as a result of what the German law classified as consent between two adult males. Party A agrees to eat while Party B agrees to be eaten. Was it manslaughter, murder or euthanasia? Defence pleads assisted suicide, Prosecution argues erotic domination. The "contract" arises via a digital doorway between two men in their forties. The "eater" (one cannot say the "perpetrator", because both were purportedly agents) had always wanted a brother whom he wanted to consume, in order to bind them together forever. That was his defence. It suggests a woeful ignorance of biological processes. The digestive processes would dispense with that delusion. Nothing at all like transplantation.

The "eatee" was obsessed with the story of Hansel and Gretel. That can't be all there is to it. A children's story is surely not sufficient cause to persuade a young man (even if he is made of gingerbread) to allow himself to be devoured by a stranger.

9:

REMEMBER THE NOTION of the *willing seller?* These are the terms of my negotiation with Viv. She is not so much willing, as eager. I watch her contained excitement as I tentatively propose a most immodest proposal. Then she chuckles.

"*Ja, vok, ja*. I doesn't mind. I want to buy me a nice digital video camera." Viv makes an almost instant calculation. One kidney in exchange for a universe of visual play. Perhaps in three years time when the camera lies unused at the back of her cupboard, she might think of it as an unequal exchange.

I am quietly elated. Obviously I had a great fear that this encounter would come down to an act of coercion. That was never the plan. I have no taste for domination. Insinuation is more my style. My man is sure that there will be no complications and that Viv will end up living a pain-free existence with one healthy kidney. Probably she also will be able to visit the uncle and aunt who settled in Australia with the other economic migrants and political exiles who no longer know which they are. The recipient of the kidney, who even at this late stage in the drama waits off-stage in the wings, would by then be living a liberated existence somewhere or other, free of the continuous enslavement to the dialysis machine. I would be freed of my debt to my brother. Those of you who do not carry such a burden will not comprehend its weight. So it is for my sake as much as Viv's that I make sure that her consent is informed. I cannot compound my debt.

"You must understand, Viv, that every consideration will be taken for you to experience no inconvenience or risk. Your generosity will be rewarded. You will come to no harm. I cannot of course guarantee this, but I can guarantee, Viv, that this will be my objective."

I describe the recovery period; I explain a few aspects of the procedure; something of my own story. My brother's name comes into it once or twice. At a certain point it is clear that once the financial negotiation is secured, she cares only about a single piece of information.

"It will be clean, hey? I doesn't want me to get sick."

She means the surgery.

It is the same question which all recipients ask their agents. They have heard some worrying statistics about South Africa.

Do you remember Mr Darvall? Bossie Bosman persuaded him to give his daughter's heart to a stranger. Not a perfect stranger. Not a complete stranger. Louis Washkansky was an incomplete and imperfect stranger who needed Denise's heart. The unimaginable was granted. The father gave away his daughter's heart in a contract of good faith.

I am not a father myself, but am not without paternal instincts. It seems reasonable that I can offset any personal discomfort that Viv may experience by seeing to it that she gets enough money to buy herself a good DVD camera as well as an air-ticket to visit Australia. Many young women are paid pretty poorly to have some unknown person inside of them in very unhygienic circumstances. The father is often the broker in such deals. Here I was willing to pay this young woman (rather handsomely) to have part of herself placed inside some unknown person under hygienic conditions.

Viv's kidney will not be stolen. It is a gift, and one that has been paid for. My conscience is clear, and it fills me with hope that I may have found a system that strengthens the bond we all have with one another. Perhaps that is the ideal for which Chris had been working all along.

10:

Dr — regrets that he is otherwise contracted for the next four days. An international *obligation*, his unctuous tone advises. "Please to prep the donor in advance. No food from the evening of the third day."

"What do I do until then?" Mild panic at the idea of the infinite time ahead.

"You will have to learn how to muddle along together," he tells me. Tasks. The time will be taken up with tasks. Have that electric fence installed.

That will reduce the risk of unintended visitors to my property. The activity absorbs most of day one. Mrs Peters, who "does" three days a week, is given an early annual leave. Would she imagine Viv to be my concubine or an illegitimate daughter?

It was all I could do to persuade the girl to keep herself concealed in my study for the first twelve hours of her voluntary captivity. Then her prattling self is everywhere in the house, full of curiosity, needs, appetites. She goes into things. My fridge. Could she have boiled eggs for breakfast – soft, with white toast? My kitchen cupboards. What is the difference between vanilla essence and vanilla extract? My study. Who is going to get all my books when I die? She seems unaware which of these questions is rude, which naïve, which adorable. Apparently there is some concern about the impending surgery. She tries to read my papers on Chris, which I am eager to show her. Surprisingly, a strong reader, she lets me know that the Barnard documents are not what she is looking for.

"Never heard of him." She knows nothing of the heart transplant in South Africa. That comes as no shock to me. But she is interested in my files on the history of the kidney transplant. I have plenty of evidence for her of the successes. It seems unhelpful to show her any of the more worrying information, and there is no sign that she seeks that more complex understanding.

Is hers the natural optimism of the young? She has the greedy pleasures of a precocious child. Loitering about the house, leaving empty toffee wrappers like breadcrumbs at strategic points (beside the phone, next to the toilet, near the kettle), she marks her trail, signals her day's activities for me to discover on returning from those of the Tasks which take me out into the world. Most of my time, I spend getting her pharmaceutical supplies and small indulgences: magazines, drinking yoghurt, lip-ice, toffees, tampons. She sleeps a lot. She watches television. We are becoming habituated to one another. An evening is passed sitting laughing at a dance competition together. Scrunched up on the sofa, her back toward me. Her midriff is bare, and I imagine where the knife will enter. I am aware of her as little more than a membrane containing her secret inner self.

I discover that I want to be inside her.

That is of course my medical curiosity, but it has a strangely sad strong power.

I have become impure of heart. That is all it takes. Those of you who have not lived on a threshold will have difficulty understanding the power of such definitions for the human heart. The plan has become impossible. I am not pursuing this for Viv or for the abstract good. I have been taken over by a compelling possessive desire. That is enough to make her undesirable.

It takes all of my will to instruct her to leave. What I need to do cannot be contaminated, or it will have no validity. There must not be more in the transaction than I had banked on. This gift could not be for me, or it would increase, not cancel, my debt.

"I'm sorry, but you will have to go. Now. Please go."

At first she cannot understand what it is that I am saying. Then her disappointment expresses itself as fury. She is offended.

"So what's wrong with me?" She flounces with the wounded dignity of a rejected lover, slams doors. It takes some bullying to convince her that I am serious. I hear her sobbing in the bathroom, where she tries to make herself vomit.

I try to explain myself, but that produces a ridiculous and incomprehensible series of falsehoods because I have, of course, withdrawn from relationships of intimacy before now. Stumbling without anyone in charge of the situation, my tongue produces one alibi after another. Grasping for a credible justification, I finally assert,

"Look, I can't send you back onto the street with a wound in your side. It's too – it's too *biblical*." Who had produced that idea? Was it Chris? Chris's father talking? Then I come to myself.

140

"What if something goes wrong. You know where I live." That logic had not occurred to me before, but she understood it immediately.

"I signed a consent form," she snivels from behind the bathroom door, with all of the legal authority of a TV viewer.

"That, my dear girl, is not worth the paper it is written on."

In the end, after several hours of cajoling (mine) and protests (hers), my will prevails. But she is only stilled when I give her the contact number for the doctor. She is determined, I think, to embark on the dark journey alone. It is well after sunset when I drive her to the railway station. Over her shoulder is a piglet backpack which had been my parting gift to her. Perhaps it is a metaphor.

Then there is the calm of simple activity. I remove all traces of Viv – the toffee wrappers, the puerile magazines, cream-soda drinking yoghurt. No one would ever be able to demonstrate that she had even existed. Just as well. If she were to have an untoward encounter with the doctor, there would be nothing to link us. For one thing, how would she have got in? As my house recovers itself, I am flooded with euphoria. Anything may be achieved. My mind becomes clear.

You had led yourself astray. The only immaculate donation would come from your brother. Substitutions are not possible.

At last, you feel the spirit of Bossie Bosman descend upon you.

141

Other fiction titles available from Jacana

Counting Sleeping Beauties
Hazel Frankel

Blood's Mist
David Donald

Shiva's Dance
Elana Bregin

Black Petals
Bryan Rostron

Coconut
Kopano Matlwa

The Sunburnt Queen
Hazel Crampton

For a complete list of Jacana titles, visit www.jacana.co.za